VAMPIRE HUNTER

SILVERWOOD ACADEMY
BOOK ONE

ID JOHNSON

For Nancy. You are a badass.

CONTENTS

1

EARTH SHATTERING

Rachael

THE CURSOR on the laptop continued to blink at her expectantly, even though Rachael Barnes couldn't think of a single word to type. "Shit," she muttered under her breath, realizing the pen she'd been chewing on was also useless at this point. Scrappy, her calico, American short-hair, rubbed up against her leg, but Rachael didn't pull her eyes away from the damn blinking beacon. "In a minute, kitty." She had to write three hundred more words in the next couple of hours to meet her deadline, and if she didn't, there were going to be a lot of angry WebReader fans across the world. This was no time to screw around.

"What happens next?" she asked, tossing the pen into the air as if it might clatter off the table and give her some sort of indication of what her main characters should do now. Of course, that was also no help, so Rachael dropped her head onto the desk, evading the keyboard, and letting out a sigh. Not for the first time in the last week, she was regretting killing off her heroine.

Sure, she'd been able to stretch out the grieving amongst the rest of the cast enough to fill her quota for a few days before she'd had to figure out a new plot line. At the time, as Chell Knight lay dying in her fiancé's arms, it had all seemed so clear. It was time for Chell to go, for the other characters in the Silverwood Academy series to take flight. After all, Chell was taking up so much screen time, and as much as Rachael loved her, she'd become a crutch to Rachael's writing. She needed to find a way to make her story interesting without Chell.

More importantly, it had been huge for ratings. Over a million people had read Episode 574 within hours of its posting. Even on her best days before that, Rachael had been pulling in shy of 700,000. Since then, her views had continued to grow so that Silverwood Academy was by far the most popular series on WebReader, which was the most popular novel series site in the world. Killing off Chell would be worth it if she could sustain those kinds of numbers. A few more months with that sort of following, and her next commission check would be enough to put a down payment on a house--*a house!* She could finally move out of this shitty apartment and prove to her mother that quitting her accounting job to concentrate on her writing full-time really had been the best decision.

It was obvious now that she hadn't been prepared, though, and the readers were starting to let her hear about it. One thing was certain, the patrons of WebReader were a vocal bunch, and while she'd been getting mostly positive comments for the last two years since she started writing the saga, now, more and more of the feedback was angsty. "Why'd you kill off Chell if nothing cool is going to happen?" Or, "Is everyone going to stop crying one of these days? What happens next?" her readers wanted to know.

Shaking her head, Rachael said aloud, "Good question, XiYon54. Don't we all want to know?"

Eventually, she'd planned on working the plot out so that Chell's fiancé, the dark and brooding Graham Halloway, would find a new love interest in a new character, a new student at Silverwood Academy. But she realized too late that it would take far too long to introduce a new woman into Graham's life--and that would also shift the emphasis on the story to him. Sure, she could highlight Chell's older sister, Sammi, but she'd already made her a bit of a dark horse, and the last thing she needed was for people to end up hating her main character.

"Surely, I can come up with three hundred more filler words and worry about this tomorrow....." Rachael read back over what she'd just written. Professor Jared McCall, one of Chell's good friends and another of Rachael's secondary characters that fans seemed to really like, was lecturing his class. He was telling them how important it was to be completely prepared when entering a fray with a bloodsucker when a student asked a question that brought back a memory of Chell, and the professor had fled the room in tears. Rachael was considering having him run into someone in the hallway, maybe this new student, but it just didn't seem to be working. Who was this girl? Where was she from? Why was she starting class in the middle of the semester? "And what the hell is her name?"

"Meow," Scrappy called again, clawing at Rachael's leg, gently, but annoying just the same.

Shaking the cat off, she said, "Quit. You've got food and water. Give me ten minutes.... Twenty minutes." It wasn't like her kitty to be so agitated. Scrappy scratched a little harder this time, and Rachael wished she'd been wearing pants because it kind of hurt. She glanced down at the ratty gym shorts she'd thrown on that morning and pondered going to change into leggings or jeans. But she was going to take a shower and get cleaned up to have lunch with a friend as soon as she was done with this episode and submitted it to her editor, Lark. So focus was key. She could do this--power through. Write a few more sentences, and get the hell out of there. Then, she could shower, change, and go meet Ebony for lunch.

With an air of decisiveness she didn't feel in her heart, she declared, "Fine. Jared will meet this chick in the hall. She can just be generic for now. We don't even need a last name at a first meeting. No explanation necessary. The good prof is upset; he's taking a minute to collect himself. New girl wanders by--lost. He points her in the right direction, and runs back inside to apologize to the class and say they can go a few minutes early. Easy enough." Satisfied that she could stretch that into three hundred words, Rachael poised her fingers over the keys.

The words started flowing again, enough of them anyway. She got there--three hundred and five words. Good enough for her quota. Good enough to send in to her editor who would read through it quickly enough, make any corrections to typos, and then stick this sucker up for her adoring fans. She hadn't even needed to send Jared back into his classroom to get her words in and craft a satisfying conclusion to the episode. All was well with the world.

And then that damn Professor McCall had to go and ask a stupid ass question. "I don't think I caught your name, miss. What is it?"

"Why'd you say that?" Rachael cursed her own character for speaking out of turn, something they did often enough, even though it was technically her fingers flying over the keys.

She had no idea what the answer to the question might be. But thinking about the fact that she wrote under a pen name and needed a name quickly, she chose her own name, her real name, for now, and typed it in.

"Oh, uh, I'm Rachael," the girl said. "It's nice to meet you."

"You, too," Professor McCall said with a smile. "It's very nice to meet you, too, Rachael."

With a deep breath, Rachael ended the episode, closing the document with a satisfied smile. "All I have left to do is send this to Lark and...."

Rachael stopped mid-sentence as the floor beneath her feet began to vibrate. Dishes in the cabinets rattled, knickknacks shifted slightly on their shelves, even the books seemed to be dancing.

"Merreow!" Scrappy screeched, her tail up and all of the hair standing on end across her back.

Bracing her palms against the table, Rachael tried to imagine what could possibly be making her second-story apartment shake. "We don't have earthquakes in Baltimore, do we?" she asked, her eyes wide with alarm.

As quickly as it had started, the rumbling ended, and everything went still. Scrappy seemed to relax slightly, but Rachael didn't move, not yet.

Once she was sure the ground beneath her feet was solid, she stood and crossed over to the window. A look outside told her nothing. Cars continued to pass on the highway, I-95, a half mile from Shady Side Apartments. The trees and green spaces all looked normal. She didn't hear any sirens or people screaming. "Huh…."

Rachael walked to the front door and opened it slightly, sticking her head out into the open space near the stairs that led to the ground. There were four apartments here, two across from hers and one beside. She could hear a TV laugh track coming from one and music from another. The other was silent, but in the parking lot at the foot of the stairs, she heard some people talking, and by the tone of their conversation and soft chuckling, she thought they seemed unbothered. The concrete didn't appear to be cracked. She didn't smell gas or see anything at all unusual.

"Weird." She pulled her head back in and closed the door before Scrappy had a chance to dart out, not something she usually did, but under the circumstances, Rachael wasn't taking any chances. Weird cat. Weird shaking. Just plain weird.

Shaking her head, she crossed the room. "Maybe I imagined it." She knew that wasn't the case. There were a few glass collectibles on her shelf that had moved out of their positions, and a vase on her writing table that held silk flowers from her coworkers on her last day at Merek and Merek that had moved as well.

"Whatever." She shook her head again, deciding it must not be anything to worry about. Maybe an airliner took off at the airport a few miles away, though that had never shook the apartment before. Or maybe a big truck had gotten off the highway at the closest exit and that had rattled the building. She didn't have time to think about it at the moment. If she was going to make her lunch with Ebony, she'd have to hurry.

Rachael flipped open her laptop and quickly sent the email to her editor before heading off to take a shower, hoping whatever that rattle had been it hadn't broken any pipes or affected the hot water heater. Nobody liked a cold shower.

2

WEIRD LUNCH

Rachael

RACHAEL CLIMBED into her SUV and barreled out of the parking lot, hoping the estimate on her phone of how long it would take her to get to Newkirk Street was off. Normally, she would've left ten minutes earlier because she hated being late and liked to give herself plenty of time. But those damn characters hadn't been so cooperative today.

Trying not to think about her story, Rachael let her mind wander back to college. She turned on her blinker and changed lanes, thinking about her good friend Ebony and wondering if she'd left the office yet. She'd probably change into sneakers and walk the half-mile to Karella's knowing Ebony and her need to make sure she got her steps in every day. Rachael smirked. If only some of that willingness to exercise had worn off on her when they were college roommates.

Ebony Gibbons had been one of Rachael's closest friends since they'd met in an accounting class their freshman year and decided to be roommates from their sophomore year until they both graduated with bachelors in accounting from the University of Maryland. The outgoing Ebony had taken Rachael under her wing even before they'd moved in together, making sure Rachael got a taste of all college life had to offer, and when Ebony had gotten a paid internship at Merek and Merek her senior year, she'd managed to get Rachael a position, too, which eventually led to them both being hired as junior accountants right out of college. While Ebony thrived under the high pressure Frank and Joe Merek kept on their employees, Rachael had floundered out of the gates, realizing about four years too late she'd picked the wrong major. Though she was good at math, she had never been passionate about it like Ebony, but had let her parent's insistence that accounting was a financially sound choice sway her thinking. She'd always wished she'd chosen something where she was allowed to be more creative.

With five minutes to spare before she'd be late, Rachael turned onto Newkirk. The restaurant was still a few blocks away. She prayed the lights would be cooperative.

Almost from the start of her official, full-time, salaried employment at Merek and Merek, Rachael had spent her days dreaming of getting out from under the brothers' thumbs. Instead of focusing on her work, she'd spent most of her time daydreaming about vampires and witches, creating her own worlds in her mind in order to escape the one she found herself in on a daily basis. Any time she had a chance, she'd secretly write on the story while her coworkers were either busily working on accounts for the firm or out to lunch. While Rachael's accounting skills were enough to get her by, for the most part, she was the type of employee that never excelled and seemed to skate by with the bare minimum. Her slacking was never enough to get her fired, but she wasn't exactly a stand-out either. In the meantime, Ebony had made it out of the ranks of junior accountant to her own office with a secretary in just two years and was poised to become an officer of the company before she hit thirty.

And that had been when Rachael decided it was time for a change.

Not that she didn't love her friend or that she wasn't happy for her. She was ecstatic that Ebony was doing so well. But Rachael longed for a job that gave her the same satisfaction she saw on

Ebony's face whenever she figured out a particularly difficult problem. Rachael needed work that lit her face the way that she'd witnessed Ebony beam about a payroll spreadsheet calculated correctly or an earnings report with precise trends.

So Rachael had decided to take the story she'd been working on for years in her spare time and make the plunge into web novel writing, praying she'd somehow manage to earn enough money to quit Merek and Merek.

It hadn't happened overnight, but it had happened, and now Rachael's story was one of the most popular novels on the Internet. Thinking of that made her smile, and she was pretty sure her face was glowing as much as Ebony's did when she was figuring out a budget issue.

Rachael glanced at the time but didn't feel that bad seeing she was only five minutes late. Ebony would understand that work had called, and she'd had to stay and finish.

She pulled her blue Infiniti QX60 into an empty parking spot in a lot just down from the cafe where she was meeting Ebony and checked her lipstick in the mirror. She'd dressed in a hurry since she'd nearly ran out of time, but she thought her black slacks and cute red top were appropriate, and she looked nice. "I wonder what Rachael the student would be wearing…." Shaking her head, she tried not to get lost in her fictional world and took a deep breath to clear her mind. Still, she couldn't help but hope her characters would have something interesting to tell her tomorrow and that everyone would cooperate a little more than Jared and this new Rachael chick had today. Deciding her lipstick looked fine, she grabbed her bag and shoved her keys inside before she hopped out and clicked the lock.

Power walking wasn't really her thing, so she sent Ebony a quick text to let her know she was there but it would take a minute for her to reach the restaurant. There was no doubt in Rachael's mind that her friend had already gotten them a table. Ebony was never late.

She was busy, though, and easily distracted. So maybe she'd appreciate the fact that she'd have a chance to answer some work emails while she waited for her tardy friend. Or maybe she'd be royally pissed that Rachael was being so inconsiderate. She'd find out in a minute. Karella's familiar blue and brown striped, canopied entryway came into view as she rounded a corner, hurrying her steps a bit so Ebony would at least assume she was trying to be there on time. They'd had lunch here dozens of times in the two years they'd worked down the street at Merek and Merek together, but since Rachael had quit, they'd only had a chance to catch up a few times, so surely Ebony would be so happy to see her, she wouldn't mind that she was a few minutes late.

The expression on her friend's face said otherwise. Rachael stopped just inside the door, brushing her long, dark hair over her shoulder as she stared into narrowed brown eyes.

Ebony was sitting at a small, circular table in the middle of the restaurant, her legs crossed, foot swinging, a scowl on her face and her phone in her hand as if she were about to send a text. "You're late."

Gulping, Rachael took a few steps forward, wondering why in the world her friend was so upset. It was only five minutes…. "Sorry."

Ebony huffed and put her phone down, and Rachael took a seat, praying this was not an indication of how the rest of lunch would go because if she wanted to be yelled at, she just would've stayed home with her characters.

3

ANGRY EBONY

Rachael

GRASPING her straw between two fingers, Ebony made a point of taking a sip of her tea as she eyeballed Rachael overtop of the glass. "Really, Rach. I don't know what's gotten into you lately," she said, setting the drink aside. "I know you've been distracted, but Frank couldn't even find you this morning, and when I called, you didn't answer, not even your cell."

Rachael tipped her head to the side, confusion washing over her. Not much of what Ebony had just said made any sense at all. Before she could ask for clarification, the waitress came over. A petite blonde with bright white teeth, she seemed a little more cheerful than anyone should be before 5:00 cocktails. "Hi! I'm Marie. What can I getcha?"

One of the reasons Rachael loved this cafe more than most others in the area was because it was a table service, but at the moment, she could've done without the interruption.

She hadn't even looked at the menu yet, though she was familiar with what was on it. On the way over, she'd been considering ordering something new, but since Marie's beaming smile was starting to sear her eyeballs, she just ordered her usual. "I'll have the chicken club, chips, and a Diet Coke, please."

"Sure thing," Marie said, making no notation but grabbing the menus off the table and bouncing away.

When Rachael turned back to Ebony, she had her phone in her hand and was scrolling, murmuring to herself about which emails were important, and which weren't. "You've got to be kidding me!" she exclaimed pressing on her phone with one finger like she was trying to jab a spear through a fish. "We lost the Stenzel account?" Ebony slowly shook her head, her eyes wide, and then she read through the entire email quickly under her breath. When she was finished, she huffed and slammed her phone down on the table. "I can't believe this."

"Sorry," Rachael said, trying to sound sympathetic. She'd worked on the Stenzel account back when she was still employed at Merek and Merek, so she knew it was a lot of money, but Mr. Stenzel was such a pain in the ass to deal with, she sort of felt glad for whoever just unburdened themselves from that guy.

"I'm gonna have to get back to the office." Ebony grabbed her glass and took a long drink. "See, hon, this is why you should've been on time. I had a few things I wanted to tell you about, but now I can't because I have work to do." She placed her glass back on the table and picked up her giant, burgundy Michael Kors bag from beneath the table, shoving her phone inside. Rachael wasn't surprised to see the bag matched her shoes perfectly, and the accent color complimented her gray and black pencil skirt and slate top. She really was a snazzy dresser.

Ebony took some money out of her wallet and tossed it on the table. While no one had brought the bill yet, it was definitely enough to cover her part. Standing, she added, "You should think about getting back to work, too. Did you already take a lunch before this one? Why weren't you here at 12:00? You should at least call Frank back. He's already pretty pissed you weren't there this morning. Where were you anyway?"

Rachael watched the whirlwind in front of her, considering

whether or not she should protest Ebony leaving. She had just driven all the way downtown to have lunch with her friend. But then… if Ebony was going to act all weird and yelly, did she even want to see her? So many questions floated around in her mind. Why did Ebony think they were supposed to meet at 12:00 instead of 12:30? Why did she keep talking about Frank? And… was she implying that Rachael did not have work to do?

Before she got a chance to reply to anything Ebony had just said or throw some accusatory remarks of her own out onto the table, Ebony's phone rang. "Oh, shoot!" She opened her bag and stuck her hand in, searching for a second before she pulled it out.

"Eb…" Rachael began, but she could see there was no sense in replying. Ebony was already on the phone, talking to someone back at her office. She took a few steps toward the door. "See you later," Rachael called, flabbergasted.

Lowering the mouthpiece so the person on the other end would know she was speaking to someone else, her friend replied, "Yep, see you back there," and then made her way out of the cafe into the throng of lunch-seekers.

Rachael followed her with her eyes until she disappeared into the crowd. "What just happened?" she asked, not for the first time that day. Everything was so weird! First… her cat had been bonkers all morning. Then, there'd been that weird shift in the ground, like an earthquake, but no damage that she could see or had heard of. And now, Ebony was acting like Rachael had shown up super late to lunch and made her company lose a major account. "So bizarre…."

She turned back around to see Marie bringing her food over. The waitress set her plate and glass down. "Here you go!" Eyeing the money on the table, she asked, "Oh, did your friend leave?"

"Yeah, she had to get back to work."

"Oh, I'm sorry. Well, lots of people eat lunch alone." She gave Rachael a sympathetic smile and picked up the bills off the table.

Rachael wanted to tell her that she was actually never alone because thousands of characters lived in her head, but she recognized the crazy before it came out of her mouth, so she ignored the remark.

"She was here for a long time by herself, too," Marie went on. "Guess someone got the time wrong." She made a soft, "hmph" sound, like she just knew it had to be Rachael, and then added, "Enjoy your lunch," and headed off to annoy someone else.

If the chicken club didn't look so delicious, Rachael might've just tossed her own set of bills on the table and left. But she hadn't had any breakfast, so there was no way she was walking away from the food she'd bought. Besides, it definitely didn't bother her to eat alone. She just couldn't figure out what was wrong with everyone.

Deciding none of it really mattered much anyway, Ebony was probably just in a weird mood, and her friend probably looked at the text wrong that confirmed they'd meet at 12:30, Rachael dug into her sandwich, getting through the first half and a good deal of chips before the nagging question began to eat at her again. There was really only one way to prove that she wasn't that late. Dusting her hands off on a napkin, she pulled her phone out of her purse.

As soon as she unlocked it, she noticed she had three missed calls and a voicemail. Since no one ever called her but scammers, which were usually caught by her fraud detection app, and her mother, who wouldn't call until much later in the evening unless it was an emergency, Rachael found it odd that she had a message and forgot about the text for a second as she flipped to her calls. It would make sense that all three would be from Ebony.

But they weren't. Only one missed call was from her friend, and that one had been from much earlier in the morning.

Rachael's eyebrows knit together as she rested her hand on her fist, elbow propped on the table, and contemplated how she hadn't known she had a missed call before she left home. She was pretty sure she'd checked her phone before she left the house. *Maybe whatever that earthquake-thing was knocked out some of the cell towers,* she thought. But... the call was earlier than that, and so were the other two, both from Merek and Merek, though different numbers.

Rachael clicked on her voicemail and waited for it to connect. When Frank Merek's familiar voice hit her ear, her stomach tightened up. He'd been a nice enough boss, but the thought of being back in corporate America was nauseating to say the least.

"Hello, Rachael. Frank here. I, uh… was just looking for you to talk about the Stenzel account. Haven't seen you. Hope you're okay. Give me a call when you can, and let me know what's going on. Thanks."

"Everything okay?" Marie was back, her smile tight around the corners of her mouth, like maybe *she* wasn't okay, and her eyes darted behind Rachael to the door.

A glance over her shoulder let Rachael know why. There were more people waiting than tables available, and she was just one person. It was just as well. She'd lost her appetite anyway. "Fine, thanks. Can I have a to-go box. And the check?"

"Of course!" Marie perked right up at the idea that she was leaving and bounded off to get the requested items.

Rachael stared at her phone, contemplating what she should do. It seemed awfully peculiar that Frank Merek would call her to talk about the Stenzel account. She hadn't touched it in almost a year. There had to be someone else who would know more than she did. Maybe the threat of losing it had him desperate to get any information he could from anyone. And of course he hadn't seen her, not for a long while--she didn't work there anymore. Deciding it was best to let the current employees of Merek and Merek straighten it out, Rachael put her phone away and got out her wallet to pay the check. Whatever was going on in the universe, it needed to straighten itself out because Rachael was beginning to think maybe she was the one that was losing it.

4

IS IT GROUNDHOG'S DAY?

Rachael

THE SOUND of her alarm blaring had Rachael leaping from a dream so realistic, she'd thought she truly was a superhero capable of flying. Now, back in reality, her arms flailed to make the annoying noise stop. She made contact with her phone on the nightstand, and after three or four sharp jabs, peering through bleary, half-opened eyes, the beeping went away. Groaning, she put the pillow over her head and wondered why she had to get up so damn early when she was her own boss?

"Because most of your readers are in China," she reminded herself, which meant her deadline of 11:00 AM in her time zone to get her words in was really the middle of the night their time--which meant readers could start in on the story first thing in the morning if they wanted to. She had no idea why WebReader kept the schedule the way they did, but she was thankful that the editor who worked for her, Lark Anderson, was based in New York City, so even though that didn't change the deadline time, it did mean if Rachael had an issue, she could call someone in her same time zone to help her out.

17

Hopefully, that wouldn't be the case today, though, and all of her characters would cooperate.

After she'd returned from her lunch with bizarro-Ebony the day before, she'd done some reading in her genre but hadn't touched her computer. She didn't want to see what her readers thought of her chapters, not after the hasty decision she'd made to basically put herself in the story. Not that she was technically this Rachael chick-- they just had the same name. Still, if they didn't like her or didn't wonder what might happen next with the new student, there was a possibility she might take it more personally than she would other- wise. So... she'd spent most of the night binge watching *The Witcher* on Netflix and trying to figure out what to do next.

The new student Rachael probably wasn't the best love interest for Graham, unless she was a non-traditional student, someone who was older than the typical new recruit. Silverwood Academy generally served as an alternative to college, so most of the students who attended were 18 or 19 years old, whereas the professors were in their mid-twenties, like Graham and Jared, or even in their thirties or forties, depending upon how good they were at killing the undead and if they'd been asked to teach. Graham wasn't technically a prof-- he was a recruiter. There were other characters who also didn't teach classes but were essential to her plot. If this new girl was going to fit in with them, she'd have to be in her mid-twenties, like the real Rachael, not an 18-year-old baby-faced chick right out of high school. In the past, a few nontraditional students had joined the cast of char- acters, so Rachael could make it work. Or she could just forget this Rachael girl and pretend it never even happened, taking the plot a completely different way.

Nature called, and while she took care of that and then brushed her teeth, she went over a few of the scenarios that had come to mind the night before. She'd just spit out her mouthwash when she realized her phone was ringing.

Finding it odd that anyone would call her this early in the morn- ing, Rachael rushed into her bedroom and picked up her phone off the bed where she'd dropped it. The number was the same one Frank

Merek had called from the day before. "What the hell?" she asked. Why was he calling her again? A knot formed in her stomach, and she let it go to voicemail. If his message mentioned anything about not seeing her, not being able to find her, or questioned that stupid Stenzel account, she was going to fucking launch her phone through the wall. Or at least be very upset.

Since she had no place to be that day, Rachael put off taking her shower and putting on regular clothes until after she got her two thousand words in. She was wearing a different pair of ratty, cut-off shorts made of sweatpants material and a T-shirt she slept in so often it was all stretched out and deformed. But it was comfortable, so she didn't care. It wasn't like she was going to see anyone anyway. No need to fix her hair, which was somewhat still piled on top of her head in a messy bun, and she also didn't care that her eyeliner was smeared. If Scrappy protested, she could get her own cat food for breakfast.

Rachael picked her phone up and glanced at it, seeing she had a voicemail, and mumbled a curse word under her breath as she padded out to the kitchen to fix a strong cup of coffee. She was going to need it to deal with all of this oddness two days in a row.

She started the Keurig and checked her texts, disappointed that she didn't have anything new from Ebony. She'd sent her a message the afternoon before, apologizing again for being late and saying that she was certain they were supposed to meet at 12:30. Strangely enough, she wasn't able to find the texts they'd sent earlier in the week about meeting for lunch in the first place, so she couldn't prove she'd been right. Ebony hadn't answered at all, though, which was one more strange occurrence to add to the list.

Her coffee done, she poured in a bit of creamer, not too much, and put it back in the fridge before she carried the steaming cup and her phone into the little table where she did her writing. Her laptop was sitting there, closed, but if it could wear an expression, she would have to say she felt taunted, as if it were telling her today would be no different than the last several days, and no one would be cooperating with her.

She set her coffee aside and flipped the computer open, deciding to listen to the idiotic voicemail while she waited for it to find the WIFI and connect. The sound of Frank's annoyed voice hit her ear and immediately made her stomach cramp.

"Rachael… it's Frank. It's, uh, 8:30, and I haven't seen you yet this morning. Ebony said she thought you weren't feeling well yesterday and that's why we never spoke. I'm going to need you to go ahead and call me as soon as you get this, ASAP. If you're ill and need to take the day off, I understand, but I need to speak to you about the Stenzel account right away. Thanks, Rachael. Speak soon."

A wave of nausea washed over her as she stared at her phone, wishing it could do some explaining. "What the hell is wrong with him?" she asked aloud. "It's like he thinks I still work there."

Shaking her head, Rachael set the phone aside, wondering if she should call human resources and suggest they send Frank for a CAT scan. She opened her drive where she kept her story, hoping to just get into it, and froze. It was gone--all of it. The chapter she'd written the day before, the one from the day before that. In fact, all there was in her folder titled, "Silverwood Academy" were the notes she'd started making years ago, back when she first started working at Merek and Merek.

Frantically, Rachael searched her computer. Sure, all of her chapters were posted now, assuming Lark got yesterday's update with no problem, but where the hell had her 2 million word story just vanished to? It didn't make sense--none of it! Gulping in air, Rachael looked through all of her programs, all of her files, but it did her no good. It was as if the story she'd been writing for over two years was just gone, and Silverwood Academy had never existed.

5

LOSING HER MIND

Rachael

WHAT WAS WORSE than her story disappearing from her computer? When Rachael went to the WebReader site, her story was gone from there, too. Not a trace of it--anywhere. Even her pen name seemed to have never existed. "This can't be happening...." Rachael muttered, her stomach lurching.

Her hands were trembling so badly, Rachael could hardly get her phone to stay still long enough to push the few buttons to open her contacts. For some crazy reason, Lark's phone number wasn't where it should be. "What the hell?" she asked, not for the first time that day. Still fumbling, she searched the WebReader site, finally finding Lark's number, not in a place where anyone who hadn't signed a contract would be able to find it. Hopefully, this was all a misunderstanding, and Lark would be able to help her figure out what was going on. Was it possible they were angry that she hadn't sent her latest chapter in on time? Rachael was sure she'd sent it, even though it wasn't in her outbox now, but maybe it hadn't gone through, so they'd taken the whole thing down as a way to show her they meant business. Of course, that didn't explain how 2 million words of world building had disappeared from her hard drive....

Lark's voice sounded in her ear, but it was her voicemail message. "Damn," Rachael muttered as Scrappy rubbed up against her leg, meowing like she hadn't eaten in six days. Rachael let out a huff and headed off to the kitchen to check her bowls as Lark gave instructions. Both the food and water bowls were completely full to the brim, so it wasn't that. Scrappy darted off for the door, the same way she had the day before, scratching at it, like she needed to get out. Rachael shook her head and tried to concentrate on what she needed to say to Lark.

"Hey! This is Rachael Barnes. Look, something really crazy is going on. My whole story has disappeared from WebReader, and I'm not sure what's happening. I hope you got the installment I sent to you yesterday. I thought I sent it on time, but... some weird shit's been going on around here, and I'm starting to think I'm losing my mind." She giggled a little bit, but only because it was true--laugh or cry. Even before she could hang up, she heard a beeping on the phone and pulled it away, hoping the sound of an incoming call was Lark. But it wasn't. It was someone from Merek and Merek. Not worth clicking over for. "Okay, just give me a call back on this number when you get this, Lark. Thanks bunches."

She hung up and looked at her phone. Merek and Merek was calling again, but she wasn't about to answer. Scrappy wanted out the door so badly, Rachael wondered if there was a giant bird on the other side, or a rodent the likes of which one might find in Manhattan. "You're not going outside," she said to the cat as her phone went off again. It was Ebony's cell.

Upset it wasn't Lark but thinking she'd better take it anyway, Rachael answered, "Hey, what's up?"

"What's up? What's up!" Ebony was in just as good a mood as she had been the day before. "What do you mean what's up? It's almost 9:00, Rach, and you're not at work. Again! Where are you?"

Rachael's stomach continued to roll into a ball, and for a moment, she felt panic flooding her bloodstream, as if she really was supposed to be at Merek and Merek and had just forgotten. Like--three hundred days in a row. "Eb, I don't work there anymore."

"Yeah, that's what Frank's gonna be saying if you don't get your ass in this chair in the next thirty minutes. This is serious, Rach." Through clenched teeth, she added, "He's talking about firing you."

Rachael swallowed hard. "Ebony, I quit. A long time ago. I haven't worked at Merek for months. Almost a year." Her eyes went to the spot on the table where she expected to see the vase, the one with the silk flowers her coworkers had given her, the one the earthquake had jarred.

The phone almost slipped out of Rachael's hand. The vase was gone.

Dropping to her knees, Rachael checked under the furniture, wondering if there was another tremor that had knocked the vase off the table completely. Ebony was practically screaming in her ear, asking her if she was crazy. There was nothing under the table except for some dust bunnies. Rachael interrupted her friend. "What--what date is it, Ebony?"

"What? What do you mean what date is it?"

"What's the date?" Was she stuck in a horrible real-life version of the movie "Groundhog Day"?

"It's May twenty-third--a Tuesday--most people go to work on Tuesdays, Rach."

Swallowing hard again, Rachael got up. "Is it… 2024?"

"Yes, it's 2024. What the hell? Have you been smoking something, Rachael?"

"No, no, nothing like that." Had she been drugged? Scrappy meowed like the devil was inside her, glaring at the door, and Rachael's phone beeped. She was getting another call. Maybe it was the insane asylum confirming her appointment for pick up. "I've gotta go, Ebony." Her voice was just a whisper, almost unrecognizable to even herself.

She could hear Ebony continuing to shout threats as she pulled the phone away and looked to see it was Lark calling her back. "Oh, thank God." She clicked over just as she heard footsteps outside of her door. They were heavy. Male. Who in the world...? There was a knock on the door, and Scrappy practically tore her claws out scratching at the wood. "Lark, thank you for calling me back...."

"Uh, hi. Is this... Rachael... Barnes?"

Lark sounded unsure of herself, as if she had no idea who Rachael was. The knocking stopped, but Rachael could tell whoever had knocked was still standing there, waiting for her to answer. He'd just have to wait. "Yes, this is Rachael. You know, your client? I write the "Silverwood Academy" story--as Maven de Luna."

"Uhm, ma'am, I'm sorry, but I don't think I've ever heard of that story before. If you'd like to make a submission...."

Scrappy lost her mind, meowing harder, clawing away, the knocking started again, Lark continued to explain how one went about submitting to the website Rachael had been using to build her empire for years, and the world began to spin.

Her last nerve yanked to its breaking point, Rachael opened the door, yelling at Scrappy to stop, clutching her eyes closed for the briefest of seconds before she opened them to see familiar lavender orbs staring back at her. "Holy fuck...." The phone slipped out of her hand, spinning through the air toward the impossibly handsome, impossibly dashing, impossibly un-real man standing in her doorway.

He reached up and caught the phone before it flew past him, a crooked smile on his face, and Rachael knew for certain she had absolutely, positively lost her ever-loving mind.

6

HE'S NOT REAL

Rachael

"Hi. Sorry. I sure hope I didn't startle you. Are you... Rachael Barnes?"

Rachael stared with her mouth gaping, not sure what to say. The person she saw before her absolutely, positively did not exist. And yet... here he was. Standing in front of her door while her cat, finally content after a full day of craziness, purred and rubbed herself along the leg of his jeans near the black leather boots she had helped Chell-- his dead girlfriend--pick out for his birthday last year.

"Is... now a bad time? I called your office, and they said you were home sick. Clearly, you're not feeling well. I should just come back... a different time." The guy wearing Graham Halloway's face took a step back, Scrappy stuck to his leg as if her fur were caught on one of those inhumane mouse glue boards, the kind that made the animal lay there and jerk around for a while before it finally starved to death.

"My office?" Of all the utterances to make its way past her parted lips, that's what she'd come up with? Questioning what this person

25

who didn't exist meant by her office? "What--do you mean? I work from home."

His perfectly sculpted dark eyebrows raised slightly beneath his also perfectly sculpted dark hair, wavy and molded to a peak above his right eye--his right, lavender eye. "Uh, I thought you worked at an accounting firm--Merek and Merek? Is that not right? I'm sorry--you are Rachael Barnes, aren't you? I have the right address?" His eyes shot to the number by the door, and then he fumbled for a scrap of paper in the pocket of his black leather jacket. He read it over and crammed it back in, nodding slightly that he'd written down the right information.

"Yes, I am Rachael Barnes, and yes this is my apartment. And I used to work at Merek and Merek, but I don't anymore. I quit about a year ago. To write a web novel, a very popular one, one I'm sure you're very familiar with, assuming whoever put you up to this went into enough detail to let you know who you'd be portraying."

Once again, his forehead crinkled, and for a moment, Rachael thought perhaps this guy didn't exactly understand what she was referring to, but then, a wave of reality washed over her, and she actually started laughing. It was an odd sound, even to her own ears, a sort of heinous giggle, not quite a cackle, but nothing a sane person could produce either. Graham stood there across from her, looking down from his six-foot-two frame, a puzzled expression on his handsome face until she managed to catch her breath long enough to speak again.

"Who put you up to this? It had to be Ebony, right? That bitch! Man, she got me good. How did she manage to get in here and clear my computer? Was it while we were at lunch yesterday?" She clapped her hands a few times and then dropped them to her thighs, realizing that she was dressed like an eighth grader who'd forgotten she had to dress out in gym and was sent to the lost and found to find anything that sort of fit and might work for dodgeball that day. She straightened up a little then. Even if this actor had freaked her out initially, he was still hot--steaming hot--and she hated that she looked like a Texas-sized mess in front of him.

"Miss, I'm not sure who you're referring to. Unless you mean your ex-college roommate. Her name is Ebony... Gibbons? Correct?" He shook his head slightly. "I didn't look at your info that closely before I drove over. I apologize. I just... I know you're not feeling well, and you weren't expecting company, but if I can have a few minutes of your time, I have an opportunity I'd like to tell you about, one that I think you will find quite interesting, especially if you've recently considered giving up your work at Merek and Merek."

Rachael stared at him for a long moment, her arms folded beneath her chest. "Still not giving it up, then, huh? Man, you're good. You should ask for double whatever Eb's paying you. Okay, sure, Graham Halloway, come on into my humble abode. We'll sit down, and you can tell me all about Silverwood Academy and how I'd make a fine addition to your team." She tried not to roll her eyes as she made a grand, sweeping gesture with her arm, attempting to usher him inside. May as well see how far he was willing to take this. She had nothing better to do after all, except to re-write two million words of her story and figure out why it wasn't published. Surely, when this was all over, Ebony and Lark would put everything back the way it was before this little prank, wouldn't they?

Except, Graham wasn't moving. He looked even more confused now than he had during her fit of insane laughter. He turned and looked behind him, toward the stairs, as if there might be someone else there, someone giving her information. "Did you say... Silverwood? How did you...? And... I don't think I ever told you my name, did I?"

"Nope," Rachael said, still holding her arm in the air, waiting for him to come in. "I'm just highly skilled in the area of mind reading, that's all."

"Uh... while that would make an awesome addition to our team, I've got to say, I've never met a mind reader before, and I've met all kinds of people."

He still wasn't budging, so Rachael dropped her arm. "Okay, lucky guess then. I don't know. I suppose I just figured it out." She rolled her eyes so hard, for a moment all she could see was the inside of the back of her head. "Look, Mr. Halloway, I'm not sure how long it might take before those colored contact lenses become adhered to your eyeballs, so if you'd like to come in and sell me on Silverwood, best get to it. I ain't got all day."

His expression shifted slightly as he took a tentative step forward. "I'm not wearing contact lenses," he said, as if she had run him through with a silver-tipped wooden stake. "My eyes just happen to be this color. Like Elizabeth Taylor's."

"Well then, Cleopatra, have a seat." She gestured at the chair across from the tattered couch she'd gotten off Craigslist, silently wishing she'd sprung for new furniture instead of a new car, and did her best to keep up the facade. He was good, and she was interested in seeing what he had to say, though for the life of her, she couldn't figure out why in the world Ebony would go to so much trouble to bring a fake Graham Halloway to her doorstep. Didn't the woman have better things to do than come up with elaborate schemes to make her think she was losing her mind?

Graham's jeans squeaked against the leather of the chair, and he somehow managed to look even more uncomfortable. Scrappy jumped up into his lap, and he stared at the cat as if it might shift into a werewolf at any moment, not that those were real. Not that any of this was real. Rachael took a seat across from her guest, pulling her shorts down slightly before she crossed her legs, trying to look dignified in her slovenly outfit. She didn't even bother to bat at her hair. She folded her hands across her knee, waiting to see what Mr. Halloway had to say, but when Scrappy served to be too much of a distraction, she shouted for her cat to get down. Reluctantly, the kitty leaped off Graham's lap but went back to rubbing against his leg, and he looked from cat to owner and then back again, bewildered.

"Now, Mr. Halloway, what is it you'd like to tell me about? Let me guess, I secretly come from a long line of vampire hunters, and the world needs the likes of me, Rachael Renee Barnes, to train with the elite professionals from Silverwood Academy in order to keep all humans safe from threats they never knew existed. Is that about the gist of it?"

He stared at her for a moment, his mouth slightly open before he rubbed his stubble-free chin. "Has someone else from our organization reached out to you already, Rachael? Or did your grandfather make contact with you before he passed? We were under the impression you were estranged from him. Is that not the case?"

"Oh, no. Me and Gramps were best pals. It sure was a terrible thing when he passed. No one wants to get stampeded by a herd of water buffalo at the local drive-through animal park, especially not when you're eighty-seven, but Gramps lived a long and healthy life--except for those last few minutes. Those were ghastly."

Once again, Graham was quiet, contemplative. "Miss Barnes, clearly I've come at a bad time. You seem like a nice woman, though a little… stressed perhaps. I could come back tomorrow, or the next day if that would serve you better."

"That's a great idea," Rachael said, standing up and taking a few steps toward the door. "I do think you should go. You should probably just go ahead and jump in your Ferrari and head on back to Pennsylvania. I'm sorry--but I happen to like vampires. In fact, I think one day, I might like to be one. I certainly wouldn't want to go around killing any of them just for sport."

She may have gone too far. He looked a little offended now. The fake-Graham paused by the door. "Miss Barnes, I don't know what you've heard about Silverwood or who you heard it from, but I assure you, we take our work very seriously." He shook his head and ran his hand through his hair. She almost felt bad for making fun of the fake society she'd made up three years ago. "If you change your mind, here's my card." He reached into his back pocket and pulled out a business card, handing it over.

"Ooh! A card! Now that's one detail I thought Eb might've overlooked. Impressive." She took it and considered tearing it up, but clearly this dude was taking his role to heart, and there was no sense in making him feel any worse than he already did. "Thanks so much for stopping by, Mr. Halloway. It was lovely to meet you." She held the door open for him and watched him head down the steps, confusion all over his handsome face.

In a way, she was slightly sad to see him go. He was awfully easy on the eyes, after all. Of course he was--she'd created him to be that way. But whoever had gone to such great lengths to find a guy who looked exactly like Graham Halloway did in her head had done a fabulous job.

She almost wanted to go look in the parking lot to see if they'd actually sprang for a Ferrari rental. Now that would be impressive. But she didn't. She let fake Graham go, shaking her head as she closed the door before Scrappy could make a hasty exit behind him.

Rachael looked at the card. Everything on it seemed perfectly legitimate, and whoever the culprit was had gone to great lengths to make it look as if Graham really did work at the exact same Silverwood Academy from her books--the one that didn't exist. "Too bad," she said, crossing back over to her laptop and pondering what in the world she was going to do now. Besides call Ebony and get her to confess. "If only Graham Hallway were real. Now, that would be a universe I could get on board with."

7

———

THE BOTTOM OF IT

Rachael

DROPPING Graham Halloway's business card on the table, Rachael dialed Ebony's number, trying to decide how to go about telling her friend the prank was over--and not that funny. Ebony answered on the first rig. "Rachael! Where. The. Hell. Are. You." The words weren't even phrased as a question.

"Still playing that game are you, Eb?" Rachael said, chuckling and shaking her head at the audacity. "Okay, my friend. The jig is up. Or is it gig? Anyway--playtime is over. Your friend, 'Graham Halloway,' just left my apartment, and while I have to compliment you on finding such a compelling actor, I really don't understand why anyone would go to such great lengths to make me think I'd lost my mind. I mean, all you'd really have to do to make me think I was crazy was… put my car keys in the refrigerator or something. I'd be looking for them for days."

"I don't know what the hell you're talking about, Rachael, but you're about to get fired. And Frank's not real happy with me at the moment, either, since I am kind of the one that recommended he give

31

you a chance. Sure, that was three years ago, but after you fucked up the Stenzel account, he's kind of ready to throw everyone overboard. Even me."

"Eb. On. Y," Rachael said, over-pronouncing her friend's name, "I don't work there anymore. I haven't in over a year. This is… crazy. You can let it go now!"

"What are you talking about, Rachael? You do, too, work here. Your desk is right across the hall from my office. There's a picture of your mom next to your computer, and that sickly little plant I got you for your birthday a couple of years ago, that desperately needs watered, is right there, too, and your little squishy ball thing you choke the living shit out of every time you get nervous. Are you feeling all right? Have I been so busy wanting to murder you I missed some signs of serious illness?"

"Ebony, none of those things are at Merek and Merek. They're right here on my… desk." Rachael looked over at where her laptop was sitting and realized none of those items were there--in their usual spots. She looked around the room. "Did you come and take them--when you stole my flowers?"

"Stole your flowers? What the hell, Rachael? Seriously, you are starting to worry me, girlfriend. Who is this man you said came to see you? Did he have a white jacket with him? Did he offer to let you borrow it?"

"Ebony, give it up!" Rachael insisted, though she could tell in the tone her friend was using that she wasn't pretending. She swallowed hard; was there a possibility Ebony wasn't behind this? "You had to have something to do with this, Eb. Who else could sneak into my apartment, take my stuff, delete my book, find a guy who looks just like a fictional character I created, make my contact at the website pretend she doesn't know me, and make me think I'm losing my ever-loving mind? No one--no one else could've done this, Ebony. It had to be you."

The other end of the phone was silent for a long moment before Ebony asked in a calm voice, "Do I need to come over there, hon? Are you okay? Should I call your mama?"

Rachael sank down on the edge of her sofa, not sure how to answer. Her eyes flittered around the room. Everything that should've been on her desk, the items she'd brought home that last day from Merek and Merek, were gone. How was that possible if Ebony didn't come and get them, or send someone to retrieve them? What had happened to her story? Did Lark really have no idea who she was? And... who was that guy?

"Rachael? Rachael? Are you there? Sweetie, I know I've been giving you a hard time the last couple of days, but that was because I just thought you were slacking. I didn't realize... something was actually wrong."

"Uh, you know what Eb... something is wrong. I'm not feeling very well. I think.... I think I'm going to call the apartment supe and see if he'll come check the place for black mold. Maybe I'm... maybe that's why I feel like this." Rachael knew that wasn't the case. She didn't feel sick, and there was nothing wrong with her apartment. Either she was losing her mind--or the whole world had just gotten tipped on its ear. But neither one of those things required scaring her best friend. "Can you please go tell Frank I'm ill--seriously ill--and that I'll be in touch with him as soon as I can?"

"Yes, of course. Are you sure you don't want me to come over?"

"No, sweetie. It's okay. I'm going to make a few phone calls, get the place inspected, go see a doctor, and see if I can go stay with my mom or someone for a few days... until I feel better."

"That sounds like a good plan, hon. All right. Well, if you need anything at all, you just let me know, okay? And try not to worry about work. I'll go talk to Frank. I'm sorry, babe. I didn't know this was so serious or else I wouldn't have been so hard on you."

"It's okay, Ebony. I know that. I didn't realize it was so serious myself until... just now."

"Take care, sweetie," Ebony said, and Rachael hung up without saying anything else--because there was nothing else to say. She set the phone aside and held her head in her hands for a few moments, trying to sort it all out. None of it made an ounce of sense. She didn't feel like she was losing her mind. She had fresh memories of actually writing her book--of reading the posts--of reading the comments left on the posts. So where the hell did it go? And how the hell did she end up with the last two or more years of her life being a fabrication?

She had no answers, but she thought she knew someone who might be able to help her sort it out. Until she could figure out what had happened, she would just have to play along. With a deep breath, Rachael stood up and crossed to her desk. Her fingers drummed nervously for a moment before she took another deep breath and picked up Graham Halloway's business card.

8

CALLING GRAHAM

"Hello?"

Rachael sucked in a deep breath, not even sure what to say. Graham probably knew it was her. He sounded hopeful, as if he had actually wanted her to call him, and the fact that he'd answered after the first ring also made her think he either recognized her number or was praying it was her. If what he'd told her was true--and she had no explanation for how that was possible--he had driven all the way from the outskirts of Waynesboro, Pennsylvania, which was about a two hour drive if traffic was cooperative. Of course in a Ferrari....

"Hello? Rachael... is that you?"

"Uh, yeah." She squeezed her eyes closed for a second and pressed her free fist to her forehead like she could somehow force her mind to cooperate. So he did know her number. "I'm sorry... I just.... Could you come back?"

He didn't even hesitate. "Sure. That's no problem at all. I'm just at the Starbucks up the road."

"Great. I'm sorry I was so rude to you." Rachael walked a few paces away from her desk, shaking her head slightly because she still couldn't believe any of this was real. She had a lot of explaining to do, but now was not the time. "I guess I just wasn't expecting you." Now that was the understatement of the year.

"I get that a lot." He chuckled softly as he spoke, and Rachael took a moment to reflect on what a nice young man she'd created. She wondered if this is how a mother felt when her son grew up to be a decent human being. "I can be there in about ten minutes."

"Great," she said again before she caught her reflection in a mirror across the room. "Uh… actually, could you make it thirty minutes?" She pulled at a tuft of brown hair that had come loose from her bun and watched it fall limply across her forehead. "Or forty?"

He laughed again, and she imagined he was probably thinking it wouldn't really make that big of a difference if she took ten minutes or ten hours. Hopefully, she could get herself into presentable form before the handsome man, who happened to be perfect for her, arrived back at her apartment. She wondered if Chell was still dead in this new world she'd stumbled upon. "Tell you what, it's 9:30. I'll try to be there around 10:15, okay?"

"That should work." She'd have to work fast, but she could pull herself together in forty-five minutes. "Thanks, Graham."

"No problem. I'm looking forward to speaking with you." Always the polite professional, she thought. "By the way, can I bring you a drink?"

For a moment, she forgot that he'd mentioned Starbucks and wondered if it was too early to ask for a margarita. "That would be amazing," she said, her mouthwatering at the idea of an actual barista-made drink. "Caramel macchiato?"

"You got it," he said, and Rachael could actually picture that winning smile on his perfectly sculpted face

"Thank you, Graham. I'll see you soon."

"Yep, see you in a bit."

Rachael disconnected the call and then shot off to the bathroom like the streak of lightning she always imagined her vampire hunters became when they were charging in for the kill. The idea that she might actually find out for herself soon enough was just too unreal to fathom, so she put that out of her head and turned the shower on to warm up before sprinting back into her bedroom to figure out what one wears when they literally meet the man of their dreams--one who's not supposed to be real.

After a shower so quick she wasn't sure if she got all of the conditioner out of her hair, Rachael dried off and wrapped a towel around her as she debated whether it was more important to have perfect makeup or completely dry hair. It was a quick argument, but makeup won out, and she ran a brush through her hair, applied some product, and prayed it wasn't too humid outside for most of her hair to dry on its own, which was asking a lot considering how much of it she had.

Normally, it took about fifteen minutes for her to apply her makeup for work and about double that if she were going on a date or out with the girls. This morning, she wanted that second look for the time investment of the first. She pulled out her tools and went to work, praying she didn't streak her eyeliner like she usually did and have to start over again. Luck was on her side, and when her eyes were done, Rachael was impressed with her skill. She admired her work for half a second and then moved on to lips.

With ten minutes to spare before Graham was supposed to arrive, her makeup was finished. Rachael gave herself a sultry smile before she took the blow dryer to her hair for a few minutes and then ran her pick through it a few times. It wasn't completely dry, but it would do.

Rushing back into her room, she grabbed the one outfit she owned that she thought said "Potential vampire hunter/love interest," and threw it on, hoping it wasn't too warm outside for the black fitted slacks. The material was a cross between satin and nylon, but they weren't too thick. They'd have to do. This was a better-than-jeans sort of moment, and she didn't want to screw it up.

Once her purple short-sleeve top was on, she shoved her feet into her best pair of black boots, the ones with the thicker--but not too thick--heel, pulled a few bangles on her arm, grabbed her favorite gold hoops and sprayed herself down with her favorite light body spray.

The time on the clock on her nightstand ticked over to 10:15, and there was a knock on her door. "Punctual as always, Mr. Halloway," she muttered with a smile. She hoped he'd be smiling, too, when he saw her transformation. He was single now, after all, wasn't he?

Rachael shook her head, trying to remind herself that she had probably lost her grip on reality a few days back. But then, if she was going crazy, she may as well have a little fun along the way.

She headed for the door, excited to see what Graham had to say and praying that, if this was all a dream, she didn't wake up any time soon.

9

TAKE TWO

Rachael

RACHAEL PULLED open her front door, Scrappy making a beeline for Graham's pant leg as soon as the gap was big enough to squeeze through, and put on her most innocent smile, as if she hadn't just spent every second she had available to her trying to make herself not only presentable but downright hot.

She knew her time had not been wasted by the way his expression shifted as he took her in. The friendly smile he had on his face when the door first opened altered to a look of confusion, like he thought he was at the wrong place, and then to awe before he actually made a little moan, sort of a dumbfounded bleat, and then he caught himself, cleared his throat and thrust the Starbucks cup in her direction. "Hi."

Doing her best to hold back a grin at his reaction, Rachael took the cup. "Hi, thanks. And thank you for coming back over. She stepped aside and gestured for him to come in as she took a sip of her drink. It wasn't quite as hot as she would've liked, since he'd had to bring it from a few miles away, but it was still delicious. She took another sip and made her way to the sofa as Graham lowered himself into the chair he'd occupied earlier.

In her rush to get ready, Rachael hadn't taken much time to consider what she was going to say to him. He was sitting with his knees apart, his elbows on his thighs, leaning forward expectantly with his hands clasped in front of him, so she had to think of something. How in the world could she possibly explain that she had actually invented Silverwood to someone who apparently accepted it as having always been part of his reality? One of them was going to end up sounding like a nut job, and since everyone else she'd spoken to in the last two days was ready to stick that label on her, she'd have to assume Graham would also give her the honor.

"This is really good." She smiled at him, stalling, and then set her cup down on the floor by her boot, certain Scrappy wouldn't leave her rubbing-on-Graham's-leg duties and knock it over. "Listen, this morning, when you came over, I was really surprised to see you."

"I could tell." It wasn't mean, more playful than anything, and once again Rachael was reminded of what an amazing man she had created. Perfect in every way, pretty much.

"Right. It's just… I wasn't sure that Silverwood was… real." That much was true. She still wasn't. Because it couldn't be real.

Graham leaned back in his chair as if that's all he needed to hear to understand where she'd been coming from. "That's not surprising. It doesn't seem like it should be. Very few people are even aware of the existence of vampires, so seeing evidence that a place like our school is real would be startling to anyone. I'm just… still confused how you knew about us. And how you knew who I was. I mean, you recognized me immediately."

"Well, you're pretty distinctive looking." She didn't mean to drop her eyes and look him over as she spoke, but it happened just the same. When her eyes met his again, he was either confused--or shocked at her audacity. "It's your… eyes. Not many people have lavender eyes. Other than you. And Elizabeth Taylor, apparently," she added, remembering what he'd said earlier.

Once again, that excuse seemed to work, and Rachael was beginning to wonder if she'd accidentally written him to be too gullible. "I see. With them."

It took her a moment to realize he was joking, but when she did, Rachael burst out laughing, nearly knocking her drink over in the process. It wasn't that the joke was so funny as much as it was unexpected, and he'd kept his face so serious. Of course he was funny--she'd made him, and she was funny as hell.

He was grinning at her as she wiped tears from her eyes. "Sorry--I needed a laugh."

"Glad I could give that to you, then." He seemed sincere. "How did you know who I was, though? That is, who told you, 'There's a guy named Graham Halloway from Silverwood Academy who has purple eyes?'"

Rachael cleared her throat. She hadn't thought it that far through. She remembered him mentioning her paternal grandfather earlier, a man she hadn't spoken to in over twenty years. When her dad walked out on her mom, Nancy Barnes had cut ties with his entire family. The last time Rachael could remember hearing from any of them was when her aunt had sent a birthday card the year she'd turned sixteen. At least it had had a five dollar bill in it.

She couldn't tell Graham all of that, though, and she had to say something. She vaguely remembered poking fun at her grandfather's death earlier--blathering something about a water buffalo stampede. While she was sure that wasn't true, she hadn't been aware that he had even died, so she had no idea of the cause. "I saw... some papers. In a stack. From... Grandpa's house." He was looking at her with a question mark hanging over his head. Rachael pressed her hand to her forehead and looked at the floor. "I'm sorry... it's hard for me to talk about."

"Hey, I'm sorry." Graham scooted forward in the chair again, like he wanted to comfort her, but he was too far away to reach her, so he stopped on the edge of the seat. "Wessley was a good man. He'll be missed."

Dabbing at her eyes as if there were actually tears there, Rachael nodded. "I didn't get to see him as much as I would've liked to, but every memory is sacred." She had about three of those, and while she hadn't considered them to be sacred until that moment, they were at least pleasant. Wessley Barnes hadn't been a bad guy--unlike his son Billy the Bastard Barnes, as her mother liked to call him.

"Do you need a tissue?" Graham asked.

"No, it's okay." Rachael shook her head slightly, trying to clear her fake tears from her eyes. She prayed Graham didn't ask about her grandmother because she had no idea if Esther Barnes was even still alive. "Anyway, I didn't know much, but I knew something. And then, when you arrived, I thought maybe my friend Ebony was playing a prank on me. I had mentioned to her that my grandfather was... writing a book." She couldn't say that she'd told anyone about Silverwood or else her grandpa would be posthumously in trouble. No one outside of Silverwood was allowed to speak about it to anyone. "And I told her that there was a character in it with lavender eyes named Graham. I thought maybe she was just messing with me. As she is apt to do."

Again, he seemed to buy her story but he wrinkled his nose a bit. "That would be a really awful thing to do when you're sick."

"Sick?" Did he mean mentally ill? She'd felt that was the case for days.

"Yeah. I called your work this morning hoping I could schedule an appointment to meet with you, and I got your friend. She said you were out sick."

"Right. Yes, I'm sure she did say that." Rachael sucked in a deep breath. "It was really more of a... mental health day."

"And you said you didn't work there anymore earlier." It was more of a question than a statement.

She shrugged. "I'm sorry. I was just messing with you. Trying to keep you on your toes. I still thought you were an actor then, remember?" He nodded, going along with her. "In fact, I think I even spouted off something about me writing a stupid book." Cover. Your. Tracks. Rach.

Graham grinned. "Yes, you did. That was pretty funny. So was the water buffalo bit. You're pretty fast on your feet."

"Well, I do come from a long line of vampire hunters--apparently," she retorted, making him chuckle. "Is that the case?"

He nodded. "Yes, you do. One of the longest."

Rachael was surprised to hear that. She hadn't invented a back-story for her new Rachael character yet, so she had no idea how she was going to fit into the actual academy itself. "So... what happens next?" she asked, clasping her hands together. "You going to teach me everything I need to know about killing the undead?"

Again, his eyebrows arched. "Well, usually I spend an hour or so trying to convince prospective students that vampires are real, that we can train a person to kill vampires effectively, that the benefits outweigh the risks, and that they should at least come and check the school out."

Considering her entire world had been tipped on its ear recently, Rachael didn't really have to think about her options. If she stayed here in this bizarro world, she'd have to go back to Merek and Merek--not an option. It wasn't as if she could start re-writing her novel either, under the circumstances, not if everything she had written before was now true somehow.

There was no doubt in her mind what she needed to do. "When do we leave?"

10

VISITING SILVERWOOD

VELVETY GREEN PASTURELAND flew by on either side of the Ferrari as Graham kept his foot on the gas pedal, even on the sharp turns, and Rachael alternated between elation and feeling like she was going to hurl her Starbucks out the window--which was currently up, so that probably wasn't a good idea. Even without taking the highways, there was no way this trip was going to take two hours, not at this speed. She imagined Graham would slow down when he got into a more densely populated area. He definitely hadn't been pushing 140 in the city.

"Are you okay?" Graham asked, his right hand on the steering wheel, his left elbow propped near the window, like he could've driven the car with one hand tied behind his back.

"Great. Never better."

He turned for a moment and raised an eyebrow at her to see if she was serious, and Rachael smiled at him. The car slowed. "No, really, I'm fine," she insisted.

"Then maybe you should dig your fingernails out of the leather before it rips." He chuckled softly, just loud enough to be heard over the Classic Rock playing on the radio.

"Sorry." He laughed again, clearly not really worried about it. This was his car, though. She knew that without asking. She'd been there when he'd bought it last year; when he and Chell had went to the dealership together. His girlfriend had said it was a ridiculous waste of money, but he'd gotten an inheritance when his grandfather died, and he could afford it. Not to mention, there was a lot of money in vampire hunting. While the existence of Silverwood Academy was top secret, enough governmental agencies and billionaires knew about it to commission protection. Rachael had set it up that way, thinking it would be the best way to fund the expensive cars, weapons, clothes, etc. her characters would need to fight vampires and still look cool. Now, she may actually benefit from it herself.

Assuming they were somehow actually going to a school and not out to a field somewhere for this attractive, muscular man to kill her....

"So... do you have any questions?" Graham asked, switching hands so that his right elbow was resting on the console. Rachael wondered if there was a way she could resituate herself so that her left elbow "accidentally" bumped his. Perhaps she was moving too fast. It was as if her mind had already accepted that this was reality now, and she couldn't hold back her thoughts of replacing the woman she'd killed off.

Looking up at the ceiling and tapping one finger against her chin, she tried to think of something she could ask. What would a person who hadn't invented the place they were going to ask about it? "Well, what's the program like? Is it a four year program? What happens when I graduate--if I graduate? Am I automatically accepted, or is there a test?" She stopped. That should do it for now.

A crooked grin lit his face. Clearing his throat, he sat up straighter, switching to steering with only his left wrist. "I usually answer all of that in the intro meeting, but since ours was... unusual, I guess I didn't cover much of anything, did I?"

"Well, that wasn't your fault," she assured him, considering a quick pat on the arm but restraining herself. Too soon.

"It is a two year program," he said. "There is no entrance exam, but you have to meet certain criteria in the first semester to advance to the next part of the program. As long as you make adequate progress in your training and have at least a C average in your classes the first semester, you'll be approved to finish. We only expel students after the first semester if their grades fall below a 49 percent average. The program is kind of rigorous, but you did well in your university classes, so I'm sure you can handle this."

"I hope so," she muttered. Of course she could. She'd have to do well on a curriculum about a world she'd invented.

"Upon graduation, there are some options. You could be assigned to a specific detail for one of our clients. Or you could become part of our operative program, which is sort of like the FBI or CIA, but instead of taking out criminals, they take out vampires. Some graduates go back to their communities and join local teams that are no longer associated with the school. This allows them to stay near their family and friends, take on other jobs during the day, and still hunt vampires. A highly select group of graduates is asked to stay at the academy to train other students and hunt the local area. That's not likely because openings are rare, but it's possible."

Rachael knew they had an opening right now, because she'd killed Chell, but she didn't say anything about that. His eyes seemed slightly misty, but he held it together. "Everything okay?"

"Yep," Graham said quickly. "Yeah. Fine. So… the program is only three classes per semester, which may sound easy, but they are all challenging. You'll always have a physical education class--we'll teach you how to fight, how to use various weapons, how to protect yourself, etc. You'll have a class that teaches you how to tune in to parts of your brain you aren't currently using. Some people call that magic. You likely have skills there you never knew you had. Maybe even mind reading."

Rachael giggled. "That would be pretty awesome."

"And then you'll have a lecture class as well. You'll learn the history of our organization, combat theory, the origin of vampires, all sorts of things. Each class lasts an hour and a half every day, so you'll be in class for almost five hours, and then we'll expect you to train for at least two hours a day. That would be in the gym on your own or with a personal trainer. We also have a ropes course and an obstacle course, as well as various simulators. You'll be given your own dorm room, which is a lot nicer than what you're probably thinking...."

She smiled because she knew exactly what the dorm rooms were like. She'd built them. In her head.

"There's a dining hall. We have some of the best chefs in the world, so it's definitely not your typical cafeteria cuisine. You don't have to eat there, though. There are other options in nearby towns. You'll have access to transportation anytime you need it. We have a fleet of vehicles of just about any kind you can imagine. Should you choose to bring your own, we've got a garage where we keep personal cars as well."

"Like this one?" Rachael asked with a smirk.

His eyebrows arched. "Yes, like this one. How did you know this was mine and not just the academy's?"

She shrugged. "Just had a feeling."

"As you progress through the program, you'll have more opportunities to go out into the field with us, and get your hands dirty."

"Bitchin'!" Rachael exclaimed, making him chuckle. "That sounds like the best part of all."

"It is. There's nothing quite like jabbing a silver-tipped stake into a vampire's chest."

Images of all of the scenes she'd written where he or Chell had done just that came to mind. Rachael nodded, but part of her wanted to shake her head. He sounded exactly like the person she'd made up. Not knowing how this had happened was going to drive her crazy! Unless, of course, she was already crazy....

Graham slowed the car and turned on his blinker, and Rachael sucked in a deep breath. She recognized the road they were turning down, even though she'd never seen it in real life before. Large trees lined both sides of the narrow dirt road, so tall, their branches touched, curling into each other to create a canopy overhead. The effect was a mysterious path that seemed to lead nowhere, and if a person wasn't looking for the road, they might not have seen it at all. Not that there was a lot of traffic in this particular part of the Pennsylvania countryside. Rachael couldn't remember the last time they'd seen another car.

They were going a lot slower now, likely so that the gravel didn't scratch the paint on his hotrod. Rachael watched in awe, her stomach churning with anticipation. It wouldn't be too much further until they'd take a bend to the left, and then, up ahead, on a small rise in the land, she'd see a familiar brick building behind a large wrought-iron gate, dozens of mature trees obscuring the view from the road. Either that, or Graham's prank was about over.

The bend came into view, and the Ferrari traced over it, Rachael bracing herself again, not from the speed, but from the disbelief. The canopy parted, and there, in the distance, she saw it. Her lungs couldn't expand enough to consume all of the air she'd sucked in as her mouth gaped in awe.

She was out of the car the moment Graham brought it to a stop outside of the gate, unable to keep herself in her seat. None of this was possible--it was all like something out of a vivid dream. But here she was, standing in rural Pennsylvania, staring in wonder at Silverwood Academy.

1 1

SILVERWOOD ACADEMY

Rachael

SILVERWOOD ACADEMY WAS JUST as she had imagined it. The main building was three stories tall with large marble steps leading to a double entrance, at least ten feet high, with columns across the front of the porch. The east and west wings were only two stories high on either side of the central part of the school, but she knew the structure stretched back fairly far, making an expansive footprint in what she would've imagined had to have been farmland just a few days ago. The school looked like it had been here for a couple of hundred years, as it had been in her story. Ivy clung to the dark brick in patches on either wing, and with the plentitude of mature trees shading the building, this place looked slightly ominous.

Rachael stood peering through the wrought iron gate, which connected to a high brick wall that ran all the way around the hundred acre campus. Constructing a wall that massive out of brick would've cost plenty of money if it hadn't been done purely out of her imagination.

Behind the school building proper, she imagined she'd see the garages Graham had mentioned, as well as the dormitory and a few other buildings. The gym was also at the back of the main building so the domed roof didn't take away from the grand facade she was gazing at now.

Gripping the iron with both hands, Rachael didn't even realize she'd pressed her face against the barrier until Graham said, "You don't have to crawl through. We can drive--if you'd like."

Red colored her cheeks, so Rachael removed her face from the fence and slowly turned to look at him. "Okay." Play it cool, Rach.

He stood in front of his car, his arms folded across his well-chiseled chest, a smirk on his handsome face, and she considered noting aloud how lovely it was that she amused him. She thought better of it, though when she realized there was already a fondness behind that amusement, as if he was already starting to like her, to think of her as part of the team--or maybe more. So rather than draw attention to his obvious feelings, she smiled sheepishly and got back into the car.

The iron gate took its time opening, once Graham had pushed a button on his dash, and Rachael wondered if he'd mind programming her car since she was awful at that sort of thing. Of course, that would only matter if she was actually planning on moving her life here. It seemed crazy! She would essentially be packing up her entire apartment, moving away from her friends and everything she'd known since she started college seven years ago--and transplanting it into a book. It was insane.

She felt like she must be insane.

The gravel drive wound around to the back of the main building to where Rachael expected she'd see the large garage, but Graham didn't go that way. Instead, he took the circle that went to the left, up to the front of the building, and turned off the engine. Rachael stared at the marble steps, following them up the porch. Every detail, even to the designs at the top of the columns, was exactly as she'd envisioned it would be. There was no sign on the outside of the building that said this was Silverwood Academy because otherwise, anyone who wandered too closely might be intrigued enough to see what this place was all about. But Rachael didn't need a sign to tell her exactly where she was and what she'd find inside.

Graham opened her door before Rachael even realized he was out of the car. Luckily, she hadn't been leaning on it, or she might've fallen out into the gravel. He still had that smile on his face, but she didn't turn red this time, only climbed out of the car and started up the walkway, Graham following behind her.

The thick doors were carved in an intricate design, and if one looked closely enough, they could see dozens of wooden stakes hidden within the pattern. She couldn't help but grin when she saw it, and Graham said, "You noticed, did you? Most people don't."

Rachael ran her finger over the outline of one of the larger stakes. "I noticed."

He chuckled and pressed a passcode into the door before pulling the left side open for her. "You ready?"

"I've been ready for years," she replied. He arched an eyebrow at her, but didn't ask what she meant by that, and Rachael stepped across the threshold into Silverwood Academy, her boots clicking on the highly polished white marble as if noting the significance of this moment, not only for her, but for all of the characters she'd created who had walked these halls before her.

Graham was already giving her important information about the layout of the building, but Rachael didn't hear much of what he was saying. Her eyes were fixated on the large portrait at the end of the hall. She knew the administrators' offices were on their right, and on their left was a lounge for instructors and a few other rooms that had to do with the running of the school. She knew that the library was a large, round room in the center of the main building, that the east wing was designated for history classes while the right was for the scientific classes he'd mentioned earlier where she'd learn to control parts of her brain she hadn't utilized before--a less spectacular way of saying that's where she'd learn to do magic.

Halls ran from both wings to the back of the building where one could enter the gym from either side or walk a bit further to exit the building altogether to take the exterior path to the dormitory. The cafeteria was housed there, as well as living spaces for the faculty and staff, and all of the students. She knew that most of the faculty lived on campus whereas other workers--such as custodial, groundskeepers, secretaries, etc. lived in Waynesboro. All of those people had been sworn to secrecy, and all of them had cover stories for where they worked.

Graham reiterated all of this while Rachael made her way down that hallway, her eyes wide, staring at the portrait. When she finally reached it, she stopped, and Graham gave her a moment.

The man in the painting looked exactly as she'd described him. Dashing with dark hair, slicked back on top and gathered in a ponytail at the nape of his neck, his face defiant as he raised one hand toward the artist, his fingers gripping a stake. His clothing was regal, velvet in hues of burgundy and burnt orange, his jacket flying back in the wind as he made his way across a cemetery to stop the undead. His black boots rose to his knees to meet his brown pantaloons, and around his waist he wore a belt with two revolvers, though it was the stake that would bring the beast down.

The resemblance between the man in the painting and the one standing next to her was evident, especially around the chiseled jawline and the perfectly proportioned nose. But what made it even more obvious that Graham was related to the vampire hunter of old was the shade of their eyes--both lavender, both sparkling, both the sort of eyes a woman could get lost in.

"This is my great-great-grandfather," Graham said, looking at her as if he thought she might already know. "He began the academy back in 1789. This building was constructed in 1808."

Rachael nodded, but she couldn't think of a way to articulate what she was feeling. It was like another man had just leapt right out of her dreams, and though this one had died many years ago, the fact that he'd existed at all was both shocking and awe inspiring at the same time.

With a deep breath, Rachael looked the man in the painting in the eye and said, "It's nice to finally meet you, Graham Silverwood."

12

MORE FAMILIAR FACES

Rachael

WALKING down the halls of a building she'd dreamt up one day, and written so much about, next to a handsome man she knew nearly everything about but had only just met, Rachael tried to wrap her mind around how all of this had happened. The simple explanation was that she'd lost her mind a few days ago and only thought she'd created Silverwood. Was it possible it had always existed, and she knew about it subconsciously from her grandparents telling her stories when she was younger? That didn't make sense, though, because she knew about events that had transpired recently--like Chell's death. There was simply no explanation for any of it, and yet here she was, strolling along the corridors, past classrooms she'd created, to a gym she'd carefully crafted over three years of writing training scenes. Graham talked the whole time as if she didn't already know every single inch of this building like the back of her hand.

In the hallway, Rachael had seen a few students, but no one she recognized. All of the professors she was familiar with were either in their classrooms teaching or in their offices seeing students, she imagined. The gym was a different story, however, and as Graham pushed open one side of the double doors, Rachael tried not to gawk at faces she never thought she'd see with her own eyes.

The trainers--some of them minor characters, but still important--were busy taking students through their paces. There were six trainers altogether, two for each group of students, though they each had more than one group throughout the day. She tried not to stare at the four of them who were working with students now, all of them instantly recognizable.

"Those are four of our trainers," Graham said, leading her inside a bit further but still out of the way of the students and their coaches so they wouldn't be distracted. "These students are in the Upper Spring group, which will graduate soon, and that's Upper Fall. They'll graduate at the end of the summer semester."

"Right," Rachael said, remembering he had mentioned how the three semester groups worked while they were in the hallway. She'd be in the Lower Summer group if she started in June as Graham expressed that he hoped she would. There were always six groups because it was a two year program with three semesters. When the next summer group started, in a year, she'd be Upper Summer. Hearing him explain it was a little confusing, and she imagined someone who hadn't come up with the process could be slightly lost, but she was with him. She tried to think of a question a new person would ask. "And the training session lasts an hour and a half?"

"Yes, but it's blocked as two hours so that students can change and shower before they have to go to their next class, if they have one."

She nodded. The students were paired up and working on hand-to-hand combat skills. Rachael watched for a moment, her eyes wide as she noted how fast they were. It was one thing to write about a battle scene where hunters and vampires were moving three or four times faster than humanly possible; it was quite something else to see it in person.

"We will teach you how to do that," Graham assured her, standing to her left with his arms folded.

Thinking about her current level of physical fitness, that statement seemed absolutely impossible, but so was everything else she was looking at, so she may as well believe it.

Graham continued. "That tall woman with the short black hair is Marcy Star. She will be one of your trainers, along with the blond gentleman whose arms look like tree trunks. That's Flint Tork."

Rachael bit back a smile. Hearing the fictional names she'd thought up for these characters applied to real people seemed a little silly now. Who was named Flint Tork? That guy, apparently, she thought to herself. "And who are the other two trainers?" She already knew the answer but thought she should do the normal thing and ask.

"The petite brunette is Sammi Knight. I know she looks tiny and innocent, but she could crush a person's skull with her bare hands if she wanted."

If it made him uncomfortable to talk about his dead fiancée's sister, it wasn't noticeable. Sammi looked over at Rachael briefly, and the writer smiled at her, but true to form, the assassin glared and shifted her gaze back to her students. It was almost as if she knew Rachael had been the one responsible for Chell's death. Or maybe Rachael was just being paranoid.

"And that's Ty Hanes," Graham concluded. "He's one of the nicest guys you'll ever meet. Unless you're a vampire."

Rachael giggled politely and gave her attention to the muscular man at the other end of the gym. He was shouting encouraging words to some of his students that were falling behind, their sparring partners landing kicks and punches that could've been deadly in a match with a vampire. They were wearing padding now, the lightweight kind Rachael had dreamt up to keep them safe in practice, but some of them still looked pained. Ty, who was almost as tall as Graham with defined biceps and dark, smooth skin, cheered his students on, his motivational words inspiring some of the weaker ones to keep going. In contrast, to his left, Sammi was shouting threats and insults. Seemed about right, Rachael thought. She was thankful she'd be with Marcy and Flint, at least for now. They were both middle of the road--not too strict, not overly encouraging either.

"I know this looks dangerous, but they are all wearing lightweight protective gear. It helps cushion the blow. We don't wear it in combat because it wouldn't just protect us, it would make our attack on the vampires less effective as well, but when both combatants are wearing it, the material absorbs much of the transfer of energy so that no one gets hurt."

"That's amazing," Rachael said, as if he hadn't just used the words she'd written for him to say to every prospective student. "It does look dangerous, and I can't imagine I'll ever be able to do that, but I'm looking forward to giving it a try." Her eyes wandered over to the various training weapons hanging on the wall and the doors that she knew led out to the simulators. The idea that this was actually reality was starting to take precedence over finding out how it was possible.

Graham was grinning like a used car salesman who had a buyer on his hook. "I think you'll catch on pretty quickly."

A matching smile pulled up the corners of her mouth as she looked up at him, knowing he meant that and wasn't just saying it because he wanted her to stay in order to fill a quota. "Thanks," she said. "I hope so."

He held her gaze for a moment before clearing his throat and lightly punching her in the bicep, like they were ol' pals. "Come on. I'll show you the dormitory."

As much fun as it was watching the sparring, Rachael was excited to see if the dorms looked as inviting in real life as they had in her head. Glancing back across the gym, she briefly caught Sammi's eyes and saw that the woman was glaring at her again. Rachael took a deep breath and let it go. She knew Sammi was angsty, but it almost seemed like she had something against Rachael, and the trainer didn't even know who she was--did she?

Rachael followed Graham out the door, wondering if she should ask him what was up with Sammi or just pretend she hadn't noticed. Whatever it was, she prayed it didn't turn out to be problematic. She had enough drama in her life at the moment and didn't need any more.

13

THE DORMS

Rachael

THE WALK to the dormitory through the fresh air was enough to help clear Rachael's mind. Sammi Knight was written to be the anti-hero, one of the good guys, but not someone you immediately fell in love with and wanted to cheer for, like Chell. Instead, she was angry and bitter most of the time, but a hell of a fighter. So… if it looked as if she wanted to punch Rachael in the face without ever having met her, that met her personality, and there was really no reason to think it was personal.

Graham tapped a code into one of three entrances into the two-story dorm building, the one in the center at the front of the building, which was the easiest to access from the gym. Rachael pretended not to watch him punch the number in, even though she already knew his code was Chell's birthday, and waited for the door to chirp that it was open. He pulled on the heavy wooden door and gestured for her to enter. "After you."

Rachael walked into a small lobby area, one she'd taken time to describe in great detail in a few of her books because all of her main characters lived in this building and came in and out of these doors so frequently. The room was comfortable and welcoming, in neutral earth tones, with a plush sofa, two chairs, and tables with lamps flanking the seating area. Rarely did anyone sit here, but sometimes it made a good sitting area for characters to reflect while waiting on a teammate or to have a quiet discussion after a critical battle.

"There's a large lounge down here on the first floor, as well as the cafeteria," Grant said, heading past the sitting area. Rachael followed, noise from the cafeteria leaking out of the thick doors she knew she'd see as soon as she walked a few more paces.

Sure enough, two dark brown, wooden doors separated the main walkway from the cafeteria on her right. Graham pushed one door open but didn't take her all the way in. "The food really is good, and it's available all day and night."

Rachael glanced around the room. It was large enough to seat about two hundred people comfortably at the round tables that filled the space, but there were only a handful of clusters of students seated here now. Again, she didn't recognize any of them. They all looked friendly enough. No one was sitting alone, and the conversations at each table hummed and buzzed, punctuated with a laugh now and again. The colors here were slightly bolder than the lobby, but still welcoming, and she'd been certain to make sure the furniture was higher-end and comfortable. "Nice," she said with a nod.

"You're welcome to take food back to your room, too, but we don't deliver." He snickered like that was funny somehow, and Rachael smiled but didn't quite get it.

Graham let the door close and led her further down the hall, ignoring the door right across from the cafe that Rachael knew led to the staff lounge. "This is the student lounge."

This room had taken forever for Rachael to get right--as had the staff lounge, where her characters congregated a lot. The two spaces were similar, though this room was purple and gray and the other was a dark blue and silver. A large screen filled most of the far wall where TV shows and movies could be projected. Seating was plenti-ful, with large couches and chairs. A refrigerator and microwave sat over to the side, and Rachael knew the fridge was stocked with beverages of the nonalcoholic sort and that the cabinets had plenty of snacks before Graham even told her. "It's not that you can't have alcohol, but we aren't gonna make it readily available for everyone."

Grinning, Rachael said, "No, that's probably not a good idea."

"And we do have some students who are underage."

"I am not one of them." She laughed, and he did, too. "It looks like a great space."

"Yeah, it's usually pretty busy in the evenings. Most of the students are in class right now, though."

She nodded, fully aware of that. "All right. What's next?"

"Let's go take a look at the dorms."

Rachael was more than happy to follow him toward the stairs.

"The elevator doesn't get a lot of use since there's just one flight and most of us would rather get a little exercise, but there is one."

"Got it." She knew that--and there was a freight elevator, too, for furniture and larger items.

At the top of the stairs, there were two doors. Pointing to the one on the left, Graham said, "That hall goes to the staff dorms. They're all a little larger and have full kitchens, sort of like apartments." Rachael nodded in understanding. A box for a pass code separated them from that hall, but she knew plenty that would've worked if she needed in there.

Graham stepped to the other door and punched in a number. "You'll get to set your own code. It's just an extra security step in case someone gets in the building we don't want to be here." Rachael remembered when that had happened once before, in chapter fifty-four, but kept that information to herself. The door chirped, and Graham pulled it open. "And these are the student dorms."

Rachael stepped through onto plush purple and gray carpet, with matching gray wallpaper in a simple textured pattern lining the walls. The doors were painted dark gray and there were a lot of them. Graham headed down the hallway, and she followed. "We try to keep students in each of the semesters in rooms as close together as possible. There are three halls." He pointed back to where they'd first entered, and even though they were out of view, Rachael knew there were doors that led to the left and the right there. "You can access the other halls back there or at the end of this hall. Currently, Upper Summer is housed in the first half of this hall, and we are in the process of moving Lower Summer in down here." He stopped about halfway down the hall, leaving about thirty rooms between himself and the wall of windows behind him where this hall came to a junction with the perpendicular hall that led to the other two sets of dorm rooms.

"So one of these would be my room?" Rachael asked, as if she hadn't already made up her mind.

"That's right," Graham said with a nod. "We have six committed students already for the summer semester, and ten still in the recruitment process. You make eleven."

"Am I your last contact for the semester?"

"You are. It was odd. You weren't even on my list, and then yesterday, I did a routine check, the same one I do every day, and your name popped up." He shook his head and rubbed the back of his neck, like he'd been wondering for days how he'd missed her.

Rachael also found the situation curious. "Yesterday" corresponded with when her life had gone all wonky, too. Had something happened to both of them at the same time? Her eyes widened as she pondered the possibility that somehow, something had caused two worlds to collide. It sounded impossible, but the evidence that something had happened was right in front of her face. How or what it was, she didn't know, but it made the situation that much more strange. Despite the oddity of her present reality, if there was a way to put things back to how they'd been before… she didn't think she'd want to find it.

14

CHOOSING THE WRONG ROOM

Rachael

STANDING in the hall in the student dormitory, Rachael tried to concentrate on Graham's words and not the idea that something had happened recently to both of them that somehow made him aware of her existence, about the same time that everything in her world had turned bizarro. Now wasn't the time to contemplate what sort of supernatural phenomenon had transpired, though. She tried to focus in on the moment so he didn't think there was something wrong with her. Especially since he had plenty of other reasons from earlier that day to think there was something wrong with her.

Graham continued. "Anyway, you'd have your pick of any of these rooms except the first three on each side. A couple of students have already moved in, and the others that have committed have room assignments now. We'd prefer it if you chose one of the next two in order because it's just easier to keep track that way, but it doesn't really matter."

"Are they all basically the same on the inside?" Rachael asked, already knowing the answer.

"More or less." Graham stepped up to the room on the right side of the hall that would've been the next unoccupied room and punched in the generic code Rachael knew all of the unoccupied rooms were reprogrammed to as soon as the students from the last group moved out. He opened the door and held it open.

"Can I?"

"Of course."

Rachael walked inside and immediately realized where she was. She hadn't been paying attention to the number on the door, but she knew this room. A glance back at Graham made her wonder if he'd realized where they were when he'd picked the room. His expression made her think he hadn't noticed until it was too late.

The living room was clean, with beige carpeting and a matching sofa and loveseat. The coffee table had a few old rings on it from forgotten coasters. An empty bookshelf sat against one wall, and the TV that was mounted near the door was large enough for comfortable viewing in the space. Rachael noted it was only slightly smaller than the living room in her apartment. To her right was a coat closet. She opened it as if she didn't know exactly what it was and immediately had visions of the jackets she'd described hanging here a few times, when the perfect outfit had to be located. She closed the door and noted Graham was hanging back.

A sliding opaque partition separated the living room from the sleeping area. Rachael went through, but Graham waited for her in the living room. Three large windows lit the area well enough that she hadn't even needed the lights on in the living room. The furniture here was also nice--a queen sized bed, dresser, vanity, nightstand all in matching oak. To her right was a bathroom, and she knew it had a tub/shower combo, sink with plenty of counter space, private toilet area, and fresh, clean white tile before she even peeked inside. A linen closet and plenty of cabinets made the room much nicer than the average dorm room, almost like an apartment, maybe better than some.

She came back out and noted the large closet next to the bathroom. How many times had she mentally stood in there, looking for the right pair of boots, the right leather pants? This place was already like home to her because she'd practically lived there the first year she'd written the book. It was no wonder Graham didn't want to come in here. She glanced behind her at the bed. The red and gold linens were gone now, the mattress bare, but he had slept there many times. With a lump in her throat on his behalf, Rachael walked back out of the bedroom.

Graham was leaning against the back of the sofa, a solemn expression on his face, though she noticed he tried to perk up when she came in. "Well, what do you think?"

"It's great," she said smiling at him, though not exuberantly, considering how he was feeling. "What is your pet policy?"

That got a small grin out of him. "Normally, we don't allow pets in student dorms, but I think we can make an exception for Scrappy."

"She loves you," Rachael reminded him.

"I noticed." They both chuckled for a second before Rachael's eyes wandered back over the space. She couldn't believe any of this was real, but this was soberingly so. "You can have a few days, a week or so, if you need it, to think about it."

"Oh, I don't need to think about it," Rachael found herself saying. "I definitely want to do it." What was the alternative? Go back to Merek and Merek? Without him even mentioning salary, she knew this job paid way better than that one, even as a student. And besides, this was the chance of a lifetime.

"Great!" He perked up with that news. "That's amazing. We're so glad to have you, Rachael."

He stood then, and Rachael felt a little awkward, but when he wrapped his arms around her and squeezed her tight, she couldn't help but melt into him a little, even if her brain was shouting at her that this wasn't anything romantic--it was just his typical "welcome to the club" hug.

Nevertheless, she took a deep whiff of leather and spicy aftershave and felt her head spinning. Graham's chest was hard as rock, but beneath her head, it felt as soft as a pillow, and his arms around her were a little too familiar, like she was finally home.

But he wasn't hers. He was Chell's, at least in his heart and mind, for now. Here she stood in Chell's first dorm room, hugging her boyfriend, thinking of becoming her. It was all crazy, yet oddly comfortable.

Graham released her and took a step back. "Would you like to see the room across the hall?"

"Nope, I want this one, please," Rachael said with confidence.

He raised an eyebrow. "You sure?"

Something told her he'd prefer it if she chose another room--any other room--but she was sure. "Yep."

"Okay." He shrugged, like he knew it was his internal struggle, not something she needed to worry about. "Well, then, let's go do some paperwork."

"Sounds fun," she joked. Rachael took one last look around and then followed him out the door, wondering how long it would take for her to change her hair color and her name so that the transformation was complete.

15

JAZZ

Rachael

THE DOOR to Rachael's soon-to-be new home clicked shut behind her as she followed Graham back out into the hallway, wondering exactly how much paperwork there would be to fill out. She hadn't gotten very specific when she'd mentioned it in the books, so it was hard to say. Hopefully, everything was streamlined. She really didn't feel like signing over her first born.

They didn't get too far down the hall, though. The door right next to Chell's old room opened up as they were passing by, and Rachael turned to see a young, thin girl with a mass of wild curls held back by a cloth headband, dressed in athletic clothes. Her face was lit by a large smile. "I thought I heard your voice," she said to Graham, her arms folded as she kept the door slightly ajar with her back foot. "You sellin' the place next door?"

Graham chuckled. "Yeah, Jazz, and I think I have a buyer."

The girl's eyes flittered over to Rachael as she tried to determine if she had any idea who this young lady might be. She looked like she was fresh out of high school, probably seventeen or eighteen, with large brown eyes and that sort of creamy brown skin that makes you just want to pat her cheek. "Hi," she said, studying Rachael's face a moment, likely trying to figure out how old she was. "Welcome to Silverwood."

"Thanks," Rachael said, extending her hand. "I'm Rachael."

"I'm Jasmine, but everyone calls me Jazz," she said, shaking Rachael's hand like she didn't do that too often and wasn't quite sure she was doing it right.

"Jasmine?" Rachael echoed, suddenly putting two and two together. She had created a list of potential students for Graham to go visit a few weeks back. Jasmine had been on that list, but she had never actually written the scene for him to go recruit her because of everything that happened with Chell. "Jasmine Butler," Rachael muttered.

"Uh, yeah. How did you know that?" Jazz asked, folding her arms again, her head tipped to the side as the scrutinizing look increased in intensity.

Immediately, Rachael looked to Graham to see if he had also noticed her mumbling. His expression was similar to Jazz's. A stream of obscenities echoed through Rachael's head as she tried to come up with an explanation. None would come to her. "Uhh…" she stammered. She hadn't been anywhere near a computer or any paperwork yet, so she couldn't say she saw it there. There were no names posted by the doors. "The cafeteria," she blurted, hoping she didn't sound as deceitful to them as her voice did to her own ear. "I heard some of the other students chatting in the cafeteria a few minutes ago when Graham showed me where it was. One of them mentioned your name." She nodded, trying to be nonchalant.

"They did?" Jazz asked, not quite sure what to think about that.

"Yeah, they did?" Graham was just as puzzled as Jazz. Maybe more so. He rubbed his chin. "I didn't hear that."

Rachael shrugged like that was his problem. "I have pretty good ears. Some guy at one of the tables. He was just saying something about the new students. I didn't catch all of it. But I heard your name."

"Huh." Jazz seemed to buy it now. "Was he cute?"

Rachael laughed. "I didn't get that good of a look at him." Since she had no idea who she was even pinning this on, she didn't want to get the girl's hopes up that it was a potential romantic connection.

"He couldn't be as cute as this guy." Jazz winked at Graham in an over-the-top, silly flirtatious way that had him laughing while he turned red, and Rachael smiled but also wanted to be defensive.

"I told you Jazz, I'm waaay too old for you."

"No, you're not," she said turning on the charm. "You talk like you're a Boomer or somethin'."

"Yeah, twenty-eight isn't that old," Rachael agreed, though she thought it was too old for Jazz.

It took longer this time for her to realize she'd slipped up again. Graham was giving her that look. "How do you know how old I am?"

Her eyes widened again. "What?" she asked, stalling. "You, uh, told me. In the car. On the way here. Remember? When you were talking about how I shouldn't feel like I'm old just because I'm nontraditional." They had had a conversation about that topic, but she was almost positive he hadn't been specific about his age. She had to sell it, though. And quit saying stupid things. She turned to Jazz, "I hope you don't mind living next to someone who isn't exactly a kid."

"Nah, I don't mind," Jazz said, grinning at her. "You don't look that much older than me."

"And… you are my new best friend," Rachael joked, ignoring the fact that Graham still hadn't said anything. She had an idea he wasn't quite sure what to make of the fact he couldn't remember mentioning his age. At least she hadn't somehow incorporated the fact that she also knew his birthday was January 19. "Did you just graduate from high school?"

"Yeah," Jazz said, nodding and smoothing back her hair with one hand. It sprang back into place. "I was gonna go to MIT to study engineering, but when I heard I could do this and take online courses at the same time, I jumped on it. I got some scholarships to MIT, but nothing like paying for my school and paying me to go to school."

"It is an amazing opportunity," Rachael agreed. She'd forgotten she'd written it into the manuscript that all of the students were allowed to take online courses to work on their degrees while they were at the academy so if they didn't want to be full-time vampire hunters when they graduated, they'd have something else to do. Most of them couldn't finish a bachelor's degree in two years, but some got associates, and some got a huge jump on finishing their four-year degree. The academy paid for that.

"You good at laundry?" Jazz asked, resting her hands on her hips now. "I saw the little washers and dryers in our closets, but my mama always does my laundry for me. She said I'm gonna end up turnin' all my drawers pink."

Rachael laughed, imagining a woman a little older than her as Jazz's mom saying that. "I do know how to do laundry," she assured her. "I can show you."

"Sweet." Her smile broadened. "When you movin' in?"

"I don't know," Rachael said, hazarding a glance at Graham. "Hopefully soon."

"We were on our way to sign some paperwork," he replied, the look on his face that said he was still trying to figure out what had happened a moment ago not leaving him yet, but at least he had rejoined the conversation. "If she wants to, she can start moving her stuff in tomorrow. I'll have to schedule storage for your furniture, assuming you don't want to keep your apartment, and if you have any big items you want to bring, we can get movers for that."

"Cool," Rachael said, not able to control her smile. She still hadn't completely accepted that this was real, but if it was a dream, she'd go ahead and do all of the things she would want to do if it was real. The idea of waking up in a few minutes had her stomach twisting slightly.

"Well, it sure was nice to meet you," Jazz said, taking a step back toward her door. "The guy who lives across the hall is pretty cool. His name is Rex."

"Good to know." Rachael smiled at her. "It was nice to meet you, too, Jazz." Even if she was seven years older than her neighbor, it would be nice to have someone to go through the program with who had a lot of energy and knew how to make her laugh. "Guess me and Grandpa Graham will go fill out the paperwork now." She hooked her thumb in his direction, winking at Jazz with the teasing insult, and the girl giggled as Graham realized what she'd said.

"Hey! I'm not that much older than you, Rach," he reminded her, giving her a playful nudge in the arm with his elbow.

It was just the sort of reaction she was looking for. "And yet you can't hear or remember recent conversations," she continued, trying to pin her slip ups on him. She went to swat him in return for the nudge, but he was so fast, he took hold of her arm before she even made contact with his and pulled her to him, spinning her around so her back was to him. "All right, you," he said as Rachael laughed, pinned against his chest with her own arms crossed in front of her. "Looks like your new neighbor's a trouble maker," he said to Jazz, who had her mouth covered with both hands to hide her snickering, like she couldn't quite sort out what was happening.

"Damn, you're fast!" Rachael exclaimed as Graham let her go. She turned to look at him and saw he had surprised himself. His face was slightly pink, and it definitely wasn't from exertion.

"For a grandpa?" he asked, still feigning offense. Graham shook his head slightly, and then said, "See you later, Jazz."

"See ya," the teen called and Rachael waved over her shoulder as she headed down the hallway with Graham, pleased that she had found a way to get his arms around her already and hoping she hadn't pushed things too far. She was going to have to give the guy a little bit of room since he'd just lost the woman he loved, but it was going to be tough because Graham Halloway was even more perfect in real life than he was in her imagination, and that was almost as hard to believe as the fact that she was walking down the halls of Silverwood Academy.

16

CHELL

Rachael

GRAHAM DIDN'T SAY anything to Rachael until they were almost to the lounge. She assumed he wasn't sure whether or not to bring up what had happened in front of Jazz's room. As far as she was concerned, there was nothing to talk about; she'd said something to tease him, and he'd reacted the way most guys would. But something about the situation seemed to be bothering him, and Rachael wasn't sure if she should start asking more questions or just give him some time. When the door that led out of the building came into view in front of them, he said, "Sorry about all the joking around back there. I hope... it didn't bother you."

"What?" Rachael asked, making a sound in the back of her throat sort of like she was choking. "Nah, not at all. I mean, I started it."

"I know." He seemed relieved that she wasn't offended. "But... I may have taken it too far." Graham ran a hand through his hair. "It's just... I feel like I've known you a lot longer than just a few hours."

"Right?" Rachael said, turning to look at him and stopping right in front of the door. Doing her best to act like the situation was baffling to her, she held up her arms and shook her head. "It's so weird!"

"Yeah. I've talked to a lot of new recruits over the years--thousands--and... I've never felt like anyone belonged here more than you, Rach. It's a little... scary, if I'm honest."

"Well, I'm a little scary. Especially before I put my makeup on."

"No, you're not. And that's not what I meant." He shook his head at her and acted like he was considering bumping her again, but he thought better of it, to her disappointment. "I don't know. I can't really explain it. But I feel like... Silverwood wants you here. Like you should've been here a long time ago."

Hiding a smile, Rachael said, "I feel like I belong here--more than I've ever felt like I've belonged anywhere before."

With that smile that could melt a girl's heart, Graham nodded and said, "Well, then, let's go make it official." He pushed the door open and held it for her, and Rachael breezed through, thinking the universe was truly smiling upon her for some reason, even though she had no idea why. The idea that potentially thousands of people may now be in danger due to the large vampire population she'd just unleashed on the world was also in the back of her mind, but she hadn't quite accepted that part of the new reality yet.

Graham had a small office in the front of the school. She followed him through the reception area, saying hello to Ms. Post, a character so minor she couldn't even remember her first name without looking back through the story. An older woman who mainly answered the phone, she sat behind the main desk and spent much of the day chatting with the secretary, Ms. Keiser, whose first name was Francis, Rachael remembered, but she was on a break, so Ms. Post was filing her nails.

Voices were audible behind some of the other office doors, but Rachael didn't really care to meet any of the other administrative staff. These people had never been too interesting to her, not even the current school president, Rod Overbranch, who had retired from vampire hunting ten years ago to take over running the campus. He was mostly a talking head behind a desk, and while Rachael had intended to make him a good leader, he often came across as two-dimensional and boring. Thankfully, they made it into Graham's cozy space without any interruptions.

The office was about the size of a large closet. She'd figured he wouldn't need much space since he was either on the road recruiting or out fighting vampires most of the time, but now, seeing his tall frame squeeze behind the desk, she wished she'd been a bit more generous. He wiggled his mouse, and the desktop computer came to life. "You can have a seat." Distracted by the computer and finding the proper paperwork, he didn't notice Rachael's eyes were glued to the picture on the corner of the desk as she dropped into one of two chairs across the desk from him. Green cushions matched the accent color of the room which was otherwise white.

Chell was as beautiful in the picture as she had been on the cover image Rachael had approved for her publisher years ago. Her blonde hair was shoulder length in the photo, caught in an ocean breeze as she stood with a surfboard in one arm, the other around Graham's waist. It had been taken on their first vacation together, two years ago, in the Bahamas. Chell had been a natural at surfing, and Graham had struggled slightly, which had been a little embarrassing for him, putting him in a foul mood. They'd had an argument, but the making up had been worth it. Rachael shook her head. That wasn't her business. In the picture, which had been taken by a friendly tourist before they even hit the surf, they were both smiling, and it was easy to see how much they loved each other--how much they had loved each other.

"Rach?"

She turned to see Graham staring at her inquisitively and got the impression he'd been speaking to her. "Sorry," she muttered. "I, uh... she's beautiful."

His eyes flickered to the picture for a moment, and a small sigh escaped his lips. "Thanks." Graham cleared his throat and then turned back to her. Again, she could see he was struggling with the decision about what to say and what to let go. Tapping the paperwork he must've slid in front of her while she was lost in the photograph, he said, "You might want to read over this while I pull up the rest of the forms."

"Sure." The packet was familiar. It contained the rules for attending Silverwood, the agreement not to discuss her studies or the confidential information she'd be given as a student there with anyone, including family members. About fifty pages worth of rules, regulations, and explanations, it would take her a good hour to read it closely, which she didn't need to do at the moment in order to sign the forms Graham was printing off. Most students didn't ever read all of it, but if they did, it was later, after they'd signed their contract and filled out all the other paperwork that went along with enrolling. Still, Rachael flipped through it while Graham filled out some forms and printed them out. When he was done, he swiveled his chair around, papers in hand, and Rachael gave him her attention.

He still looked solemn from her comment about Chell. She probably shouldn't have said anything at all, but in fairness, this version of Rachael shouldn't have known Chell was dead. Any other new student wouldn't know, so it just seemed like a genuine comment a person would make. And it was true. The woman was beautiful. He handed her a pen and started going over all of the forms, showing her where to sign and initial, and letting her fill out the ones that asked for more information.

"I put your move in date as tomorrow, but it doesn't matter when you want to bring your stuff over, so long as you're ready to start classes on the first."

"Great." She signed that form, noting he'd added an exception to the no pet policy for her.

After about six more forms, they got to the last one, the page where she had to swear never to discuss Silverwood with anyone. The fact that she'd already literally told the entire world was stuck in her mind. Remembering the comment she'd made earlier about Ebony, she asked, "What about people I've already told--like my friend Ebony? I didn't realize I was telling her anything that was true at the time." That was an understatement.

"That's why we ask for the date," Graham assured her with a smile.

Assuming that meant the agreement wasn't retroactive, Rachael nodded and signed her name. In the current version of the world, her book didn't seem to exist anyway, but the glares she'd gotten from Sammi earlier made her want to cover her ass, just in case it all came back to bite her.

"That's that," Graham said, stacking it all up. "I'll make you a copy." He stood, taking the papers with him, and Rachael knew he'd have to go down the hall to use the copy room since there wasn't a copier in his office.

Once he was gone, she couldn't help but grab the photograph off the desk, careful not to smudge the glass. "You sure were beautiful, Chell Knight," she whispered, staring at the athletically built blonde. It was almost as hard to believe the woman was dead as it was to believe she'd apparently been alive at one point. Graham looked much more relaxed in the picture than he did now, though he did hide his grief fairly well considering how fresh the wound was.

Hearing his voice nearby in the hall, and another male she supposed had to be President Overbranch, Rachael set the frame back where it had been and pulled out her phone, pretending to check social media, though anxiety about Graham coming back in the room and noticing she'd been looking at his personal item kept her eyes from focusing.

"I think she will," Graham was saying as he pushed the door open, and Rachael immediately assumed he had to be talking about her, which was ridiculous. He could've been talking about anyone.

Whether or not the comment had been in reference to her, she might never find out as Graham said nothing about the conversation when he came back to his desk. "All right." He sat down and opened a desk drawer, pulling out a manilla envelope and sliding her copy inside. "This is yours." Rolling his chair back slightly, he produced a manilla folder from another drawer, dropped it on his desk, hastily wrote her name on the tab, shoved his copy inside, and filed her information in a different desk drawer. "I keep all the new students where I can find them. Best way to keep an eye on you guys." He grinned at her, and she smiled, even though she'd written that joke herself, and he said it to everyone. "Any more questions?"

"No, I...." Rachael stopped. He wasn't listening to her. Graham reached over and moved the picture a fraction of an inch to the right, his eyes narrowed for a moment, before he turned back to face her. The accusatory look was gone, but Rachael felt bad. How had he noticed she'd moved it so slightly? Should she apologize? "No, I'm good."

"Great. Then, I'll give you a ride back home, and you can take care of whatever you need to, and then let me know when you think you might be back."

"Sounds good," she said, but the feeling that he was upset about the picture kept her from standing when he did. "Graham... I'm sorry. I just... uh... is that your girlfriend? I mean, I know it isn't my business. I just... got the impression maybe you didn't have one, but then it looks like you do." She shouldn't have asked, should've never opened her mouth, but now that it was out, there wasn't anything she could do to take it back.

He hesitated, and for a moment, Rachael thought he might sit back down and tell her the entire story. Instead, he glanced at the picture and then back at her. "She was my fiancée, but she isn't now."

"Oh." Rachael's forehead crinkled as she contemplated whether or not she should ask more. But she didn't. She should just assume they broke up then? Even though she knew that wasn't the case. Unless... was it possible in this bizarro world, Chell wasn't dead?

"Ready?"

"Yep." She stood this time and followed him to the door. Graham opened it for her but didn't say anything, didn't even look her way, and Rachael exited, thinking it was going to be a long--silent--ride home.

17

THE STORY OF CHELL

*Rachael

RACHAEL DIDN'T EXPECT Graham to say a word to her all the way back to Baltimore. It was evident she'd pushed things too far by asking about Chell, something she should've known better than to do. Yet, it seemed like a natural question for someone who shouldn't have known who the girl in the photograph on his desk was.

Maybe it wasn't the question itself that was bothering him; maybe it was the fact that Rachael had said it seemed like he was single, or that he didn't have a girlfriend, or however she'd phrased it. Was it possible he was upset because he didn't want it to seem like he wasn't attached anymore?

The landscape seemed to be flying by even faster on the way home, which made Rachael think perhaps he was in a hurry to be rid of her. She wouldn't blame him if that was the case. So far, she'd been nosy and confusing, not two attributes one usually looked for in a new friend. Rachael tried to keep her attention outside of the sports car, but staring at the blurry images was making her a little nauseated, and the last thing she needed to do was ask him to pull over so she could puke.

"You can change the station if you want to."

Rachael raised an eyebrow. Her eyes had gone to the radio just as a new song had come on, something by CCR, though she wasn't sure of the name. "Oh, no, that's okay. I just needed to focus on something else."

The car slowed down slightly. "Sorry."

"It's no problem." Here she was, saying something stupid again.

Graham didn't push the accelerator any faster, despite her assurance that he could go as fast as he wanted to. By her calculations, they'd be hitting traffic soon enough anyway, and then he'd have to slow down. It was a little before rush hour, and she assumed one of his reasons for speeding was to drop her off before it hit. But then, he'd be stuck in traffic on the way back to Pennsylvania, so was there a point?

He cleared his throat like he intended to say something. Rachael didn't dare look at him for fear she'd scare him into clamming up. A few seconds passed, a minute, and he didn't speak. She considered pulling out her phone, but she doubted she could focus on the screen with the world flying by outside.

"If I was... a little rude back there... I didn't mean to be." He cleared his throat again, and Rachael hazarded a glance in his direction. His lavender eyes were narrowed in contemplation. "I'm not used to... being alone."

Weighing a response, Rachael considered what she actually knew and what she was supposed to know before she said, "I'm sorry if I was being nosy."

"No, it's not that." He looked at her briefly again before he continued. "I can't blame you for asking, especially after...." He shook his head, and she imagined he was thinking of the flirting in the hallway outside of Jazz's room. "Anyway, for the first time in about two years, I am unattached. I didn't think I was acting any differently than I was when Chell was... around. But I guess I am, or at least I was today. It was just a little bit of an eye opener, that's all."

"Perhaps I didn't phrase my assessment of the situation very well," Rachael said, trying to put the blame on herself. "It wasn't as if I thought you were being too forward or anything like that. You just hadn't mentioned a girlfriend… fiancée… so maybe I assumed you didn't have one based on that."

"No, it was more than that." He looked at her a little bit longer this time than he had before, perhaps long enough that a driver with less talent might have had an issue staying on the road. "I told you, Rach, it seems like I've known you a lot longer than I have. I can't quite figure it out, but it's got me acting a little more friendly than I normally would. I think I probably have a propensity to joke around with girls even when I am in a relationship, innocently enough, but no one ever seemed to take it seriously when they knew I was spoken for. I'm going to have to think about that a little more now. Clearly, I've done something to give Jazz the impression I'm looking to mingle."

Rachael chuckled softly, remembering how openly flirtatious the young girl had been. "I think she just likes to mess with you," she assured him, thinking about lightly touching his arm but deciding that wasn't a good idea after what he'd just said. "Everyone else on campus knows your situation, right? It's just the new recruits who might get the wrong idea? And how many of us are female? I wouldn't worry too much about it."

Graham shrugged slightly, considering her comment. "The others know the situation, but that doesn't mean they aren't capable of getting the wrong idea."

Ignoring the fact that he was implying she'd gotten the wrong idea, which was a bit like a knife to the gut, Rachael said, "I'm sure you can set anyone straight who thinks your teasing is an invitation for more."

He nodded, and she assumed the conversation was over. Traffic ahead was building. Graham slowed his Ferrari so Rachael could manage looking out the window now.

She wasn't expecting him to say anything else, so when he did, she focused in on his words without turning to look at him.

"It's a dangerous job. No matter how hard we train, how careful we are, things happen." He was quiet, and she stole a glance at him, wondering if she should prod him on. Wiping a hand across his jaw, he dropped his wrist back onto the steering wheel. "I should've been there. I should've been able to protect her."

"Chell?" Rachael kept her voice as soft and somber as she could, glad he was finally telling her what had happened and encouraging him to keep talking.

"Yeah. We were on a job in Pittsburgh. Usually too far for us to go, but the locals there needed our help. We got a call from a former student, Stan Rider. Chell wanted to go because rumor had it these vamps were not averse to turning kids. So we went. Took our A team. I was in a different part of the building, an old Victorian house that'd been standing empty for a while, when I heard her scream." Tears glistened in Graham's eyes as he recounted what Rachael had written, how she'd killed off the love of his life. "By the time I got there, it was too late."

"A vampire… killed her?" Rachael wasn't sure if she should even say that word. How else could she phrase it? Murdered? Slayed? Ended?

But Graham nodded, unfazed. "Yeah. Caught her off guard and used a kitchen knife." His face paled as he shook his head. The scene had been gruesome, and even though Rachael hadn't intended to haunt him with images for the rest of his life when she'd written it, she understood how difficult it would be to shake the pictures out of his head. "I took him out. Didn't do Chell any good, though. She took a few final breaths, said she loved me, and then… she was gone."

Rachael did put her hand on his arm then. She couldn't help it. "I am so sorry." He had no idea how sincerely she meant it.

A shrug and another swipe at his face, and Graham seemed to have pushed the thoughts away. "Thanks--it's not your fault, obviously. But thanks."

Rachael raised an eyebrow. It was just as much her fault as it was the vampire's--more so maybe. That wasn't information she was about to volunteer, though. The idea that he would hate her if he ever found out the truth came to mind, and Rachael pulled her hand away from his sleeve, settling it in her lap.

Her readers had let her know right away that killing Chell Knight was a bad idea, that she couldn't be replaced. Now, not only was she seeing the ramifications of her choices firsthand, she was trying to be that replacement herself. The whole idea was doomed to failure, but Rachael couldn't see any alternative but to go along with it. The packet of papers thunked against her leg as Graham took a corner a little too quickly. It was a reminder that she was in this now, no turning back. The adventure, the new friends, the prospect of escaping to a new life were all perks, but the dangers were real as well. And Rachael was no longer in charge of writing this story. She couldn't help but wonder if someone else was, and if so, would they be looking for revenge against her for taking out Chell?

1 8

GOODBYE FOR NOW

Rachael

RUSH HOUR HADN'T QUITE HIT by the time Graham pulled into the parking lot. Rachael looked up at her apartment and grimaced. The idea of going back there when she could be at Silverwood was completely unappealing.

Letting out a chuckle that told her he had guessed her mood, Graham said, "It could be your last night here. If you want."

"True," she noted, thinking that sounded like a good idea. The quicker she got to Silverwood, the better the chances all of this didn't slip away. She was already concerned that she might wake up the next morning to find it had all truly been a dream. "Well, thanks a lot for everything."

"Oh, I'll walk you to the door," Graham insisted, getting out of the car.

Rachael appreciated the gesture. It wasn't dark, and she lived in a relatively safe neighborhood, but it would give her a few more minutes with Graham. Besides, there was a pretty good chance her cat would want to see him.

"Do you think you'll need to give Merek and Merek two weeks' notice?" Graham asked as Rachael gathered the bag she'd left sitting in the bottom of Graham's car all day and the packet of papers he'd given her.

It was a legitimate question. Even considering going back there for two weeks summoned bile to the back of her throat. "That would be the polite thing to do." She shrugged and closed the car door, following him to the sidewalk. "But... I really don't want to."

There was that chuckle again, that rich melodious sound she knew she'd miss the second he walked away from her. "I don't blame you. Most of the time, we recruit kids right out of high school or out of other college programs that are also finishing up for the semester. But when we do have non-traditional students, most of them elect to quit outright. Assuming you don't ever want to go back into accounting. You're probably burning bridges if you don't give them fair warning."

Rachael couldn't help but think over a year should've been plenty of time, but she couldn't have her world where she didn't work at Merek and Merek anymore and keep Graham and her fantasy world. "I don't think I'll ever want to go back there." She climbed the stairs with slow, deliberate steps, wishing there was a way to prolong his stay but knowing he'd want to get back.

Fumbling for her keys in her purse, Rachael created a stall tactic she hadn't even planned. Eventually, she found them. "Do you wanna come in and visit Scrappy for a few minutes?" she asked, hoping she'd managed to make her invitation sound as innocent as possible.

"Thanks, but no. I've gotta get back. I have a few more recruits I need to go visit tomorrow."

Her mouth wanted to turn down at the corners, despite her best efforts to control it. An idea occurred to her. "What... do I tell my family and friends? I'm going to have to tell them something. They're going to wonder why I'm moving out."

"Right." His hands were in the pockets of his leather jacket, and he extended them as he nodded, creating wings for a moment. "Normally, we sit down with a student's parents and fill them all in at the same time. But there's not anyone else in your family who needs to know about Silverwood. I would suggest you use the cover story the auxiliary staff that works in Waynesboro uses."

"What's that?" She couldn't remember ever writing the specifics about that in any of her books.

"They say they work at Waynesboro Community College for Juvenile Delinquents." Rachael's eyes widened. "It's a closed campus because some of our students are dangerous. We only allow visitors every other Wednesday and then strictly in the dormitory. Tell them you'll be teaching accounting courses. That story usually works."

Rachael's head rocked back and forth, but she thought that might be a hard sell to her mom. "Okay. I'll give it a try."

"If you believe it, they'll believe it."

She'd have to hope she could believe it then. So far, she was pretty good at believing life into things. It also occurred to her that some of the students at Silverwood were able to use telepathy to persuade people. She wondered if she had that magical ability. Maybe that could help her convince everyone she was suddenly going to teach at a junior college. Graham hadn't even shown her any of his magic--but then, there hadn't been a real need to move objects without touching them on her tour of the facilities.

Pulling herself back to the present, Rachael said, "All right, well, thanks again." She leaned back on the door slightly, and it popped open, giving Scrappy just the opportunity she needed to break out and give Graham's pant leg a good polish.

"My goodness, kitty. You are so friendly," he said, though he didn't bend over and scratch her. Rachael got the impression Graham was more of a dog person.

"She's not usually friendly at all, but she seems to like you. For some reason." She winked at him, getting a grin, but then she felt like maybe she'd been too forward. There was a thin line between teasing and flirting. Rachael might've left that behind.

"It was great meeting you, Rach," Graham said, trying to step away, but the cat glued to his leg came along. "Give me a call or shoot me a text once you know for sure when you're coming, and we'll get everything arranged."

"Awesome. Thanks, Graham." She felt like she should hug him, or at least shake his hand, but Scrappy was doing a good job of running him off. He was close to the top of the stairs now. A moment of panic struck her as she wondered if this might be the last time she ever saw him. What if she really did wake up back in the real world tomorrow?

"We'll talk soon." He gave her another smile, and headed down the stairs. Scrappy knew better than to take her happy little self down the stairs, so she stood at the top and mewed for a few moments until Rachael tossed her stuff inside of the apartment and came back to scoop her up.

Cradling the lamenting cat in her arms, she watched Graham get into his car and drive off without looking back in their direction, and she couldn't help but wonder if maybe she was just another student to him, just another recruitment job. Sure, he'd said more than once that she seemed different, like they'd known each other for years, but maybe he always said that. Not that she'd ever remembered writing that into his dialogue before. "Come on Scrap. We've got a lot of work to do." She patted her kitty's head one more time and then headed back to her apartment, hoping that glimpse of Graham's Ferrari wasn't the last time she saw him.

19

TAKE THIS JOB AND SHOVE IT

Rachael

"YOU'RE QUITTING Merek and Merek to do what?" Ebony's question was more like a shriek, and Rachael had to pull the phone away from her ear to keep from going deaf. "Are you crazy?"

"No, I'm not crazy," Rachael replied, though she wasn't exactly positive on that count at the moment. "I told you. I've always wanted to work with underprivileged children, and I think this is my opportunity. Besides, they sought me out, Ebony, and it pays more. It's really a great gig. No more rent, no more commute. I would be an idiot to pass it up."

Ebony was quiet for a few moments before she said, "Rach, the last time I talked to you, you said you thought you had black mold poisoning. Are you sure you didn't just dream this up? You've been acting really strange lately. I'm starting to worry about you."

Rachael couldn't blame her friend for being worried. She had sounded like a lunatic the last couple of days. "I understand why you'd say that, Eb, but trust me, I'm sure. I had the apartment checked out, and it's fine. I also went to the doctor, and I'm not sick. He said it had

89

to be stress. Another reason why I shouldn't return to my job at Merek and Merek." All of that was a lie, of course, but Ebony couldn't know the truth.

"Have you talked to Frank yet?" Ebony's tone wasn't any calmer than it had been when she'd first gotten the news, though she wasn't quite as loud now. "He's going to freak out."

"Not exactly." Rachael glanced down at the first draft of her resignation letter on her laptop. Her story there was different than the one she was telling Ebony now. She'd gone with the illness version from this morning. "I doubt he'll be too happy if I tell him the truth, so I'm telling him I'm sick and have to relocate for special treatment."

"Seriously, Rach?" The volume level was up again. "If he finds out the truth, he's going to be so pissed. Either way, he's going to lose it."

"Well, the only way he can know what I'm really doing is if you tell him. And--it is what it is." She shook her head, wishing she could hurry up and get off the phone. Before she called Ebony, Rachael had started tossing clothes into a giant suitcase her mother had gotten her for Christmas last year in hopes that financial independence would mean more travel for both of them. While that wasn't exactly the way things had turned out now that the world had taken a crazy turn, Rachael could still make good use of it. If she played her cards right, she'd still get to do some traveling as part of the Silverwood team, too. Visions of holding Graham's hand and gazing up at the Eiffel Tower lit up at night, stars twinkling in the background, had her mind elsewhere so that she didn't hear what Ebony said until she was shouting her name again. "Sorry--you cut out. What?"

"I said I don't think it's fair for you to ask me to lie to my boss for you."

"Oh, please, Ebony! How many times did I lie for you in college? You skipped class so often, Professor Nelson didn't recognize you when you tried to take the final. Dr. Pierce called you 'Party Princess.' He'd start off his lectures with, 'Well, I guess Party Princess couldn't be bothered with class today. Where is she, Miss Barnes?' and I'd be left stammering, trying to come up with a story other than the fact that you were hungover or hadn't made it back to the apartment in time."

"That's not true. I hardly ever missed class." Ebony's tone had changed dramatically, and Rachael assumed that was because she knew her words were dishonest. "Fine. I won't tell Frank the truth. But... you better not ask me to do anything else. As it is, I've been doing my best to keep you from getting fired the last few days. Now, here you are, quitting."

Rather than go into all of the reasons why Rachael hadn't asked Ebony to cover for her at all, except for that morning when she had mentioned the black mold, she only said, "Thanks, Ebony. I've gotta go. I need to finish packing."

"You're leaving tomorrow?" she repeated. Rachael had told her that earlier, when Ebony was still too shocked to say anything. "That seems unbelievably fast. Are you sure this place isn't a cult? Or the guy you talked to isn't a kidnapper?"

Rachael envisioned herself tied up in Graham's closet and didn't really have a problem with it. "No, I'm sure they're not. I told you, I went and visited the facility today. It's a nice place. I'm going to like it there."

"I sure hope so. It stinks you can't come back home very often. And no visitors?"

"Every other Wednesday for a few hours, but no, not really." It would be cool if Ebony came and visited her at Silverwood, but Rachael couldn't see her friend having time to trek all the way to Pennsylvania.

"Well, you be careful. If anything seems fishy at all, you get out of there, you hear me?"

"Yes, Mother Ebony," Rachael joked. "I'll be fine. I'll call you tomorrow night."

"You'd better."

"Bye, Ebony."

"Bye, Rachael."

The tension in her friend's voice was even more evident with her last words. Rachael couldn't think about that. She had too much to do. Firing off a text to Graham to let him know she would like to move herself and a few of her things in tomorrow if that would be all right, and asking what could be done with the rest of her furniture, she set her phone aside and tried to concentrate on the email she needed to send to her boss. Scrappy seemed much more content now that they were in the process of moving closer to Graham. She purred happily from her spot behind Rachael on the couch.

After a few more edits and a change to a sentence or two, Rachael sent the email, glad to have that taken care of. She'd called her mother earlier, and while she'd been slightly skeptical of the entire situation, she hadn't given Rachael any grief. She lived in Pittsburgh, so she was happy Rachael would still be close and hadn't decided to move across the country.

The property manager said he had no problem with her moving out by June 1 so long as she paid the next three months' rent. Rachael knew it was in her contract with Silverwood that they would take care of any expenses for her current housing situation. She'd read it earlier, in Graham's office, so she'd need to ask him about that, too. Her rent was currently paid through June 1, the day she'd start her classes, so she'd have to be out by then anyway.

Deciding it was time to get back to packing, Rachael picked up her phone and headed into the bedroom only to have it start ringing in her hand. A glance at the number told her it was Graham, and a warm sensation crept from her abdomen all the way to the tips of her fingers and toes. "Hello?"

"Hey. Are you packing?"

"I am. Did you make it home okay?"

"Traffic sucked, but once I got out of the city, it wasn't bad. Just wanted to let you know I've arranged for you to move in tomorrow. We set your combination on all of the doors, including your dorm, to your birthday. So just press in 1029, and that will get you in. I'm sorry I won't be here tomorrow when you arrive. I've got to head to Ohio, but I might be back late tomorrow night, maybe Thursday."

"Oh, that's okay." Rachael tried to keep the disappointment out of her voice. She'd hoped she'd have a chance to see him the next day.

"Ms. Post will help you schedule the movers to get whatever you're not bringing with you into storage. She'll need to know who your lease holder is on the apartment so she can take care of the payout for ending your lease early, assuming that's the case."

"Yep. That's great." She knew Ms. Post could easily handle all of that. "Cool." She wasn't sure what else to say. Keeping him on the phone and chatting sounded inviting, but she had work to do and had used up an awful lot of his time for one day.

"I've let one of my associates know you're coming. Tripp Cardel is another recruiter here. He's also on our local hunting team. He'll be able to help you out if you need anything. I'll text you his number in case you need something and can't find him. Feel free to ask him to carry some of your stuff in, too."

Rachael snickered. "I think I can manage that, but thanks." Of course, she knew Tripp, another of her characters whose name sounded ridiculous when applied to a real person. He was also good looking, but not as hot as Graham, and he had an on-again-off-again thing with Sammi, so there was a chance he wouldn't like Rachael if what she'd seen on Sammi's face earlier that day had been as real as it had felt.

"Seriously. Pretend he's a pack mule." She giggled again but didn't comment. "All right, Rach. I'll let you get back to packing. If you need anything, though, give me a call. I'm really excited that you're going to be with us."

"Thanks. I'm excited, too." She knew he said that to everyone, but it was still nice to hear it.

"And Rach... thanks a lot for listening to me today. I hope I didn't make you uncomfortable. It was nice to... have someone to talk to."

That--he did not say to everyone, and Rachael felt her heart liquifying. "You're welcome, Graham. Any time." She meant it, too. Maybe she could help him let go of Chell and discover there was room in his heart for someone else--maybe a spunky brunette with a loud mouth and a keen imagination.

"Talk to you soon, Rach."

He hung up while she was still formulating a goodbye, and she decided it was just as well because she'd probably say something dumb anyway, like "Catch you on the flippity-flip." She shook her head at her own silly thoughts and set her phone on the nightstand, next to a bed covered in clothes that had missed the suitcase.

A few seconds later, her phone chirped that she had a text. It was from Graham--Tripp's number. But that wasn't all. It also said, "Don't let him charm you now. I call dibs," with a winky face emoji. Rachael's face lit on fire as she tried to figure out exactly what that meant. Whatever it was--a tease, a joke, something more--it wasn't a bad thing. Perhaps she had a chance with Graham after all. She picked up her phone and simply texted back, "Thanks. I won't, lol," and then put it down, glad she hadn't tried to be clever. As long as she kept her head in the game, she might be able to pull this off. Unless Sammi Knight figured out what Rachael had done to her sister--then all bets were off.

Rachael turned back to her suitcase, a smile on her face. All of this was crazy, but it was also wonderful, and she wasn't about to miss out on her one chance at being with the guy from her dreams, even if it meant leaving her entire life behind. She'd just write herself a new one.

20

DID IT ALL VANISH?

Rachael

RACHAEL OPENED one eye and then the other, slowly, looking around her room as if she wasn't sure what oddities may present themselves today. Her alarm was still going off, so she silenced it, and then sat up.

Everything looked the same as it had the night before. Her packed suitcases, as well as a few boxes she'd managed to get her hands on and fill the evening before, all sat where she'd left them near the closet. Scrappy was meowing at the foot of the bed, wanting breakfast, and the tennis racquet Rachael had fallen asleep clutching lay next to her. At midnight, it had occurred to her that vampires were real, and if one of them decided to come after her, she wasn't prepared. Hence… the tennis racquet.

Yawning, she ran her hands through her hair, realizing now how silly she'd been, thinking a tennis racquet could stop the undead. The sooner she got out of here and to Silverwood, the better.

She padded into the bathroom, turned the shower on, did her business, including brushing her teeth, and then went back into the bedroom to get the clothes she'd laid out the night before. Even if she wouldn't be seeing Graham that day, she wanted to look nice, and he'd said he might show up later. She'd decided to wear her favorite pair of dark jeans and a red top that set her eyes off nicely. Maybe Tripp would be more inclined to help with the heavy lifting if she looked fetching.

After her shower, Rachael took her time getting dressed and making sure she looked presentable. The fact that she'd have to carry all of this stuff to her SUV and would likely get all sweaty didn't occur to her until after she was gussied up. "I guess I'll just take my time," she muttered to Scrappy who meowed in agreement.

Her laptop was still on the table in the living room, so she went to get it, thinking she should check her email before she stashed it in one of her bags. Part of her was afraid to. What if her story was back up and everything had returned to the way it had been two days ago? She knew she'd have to face reality either way, though, so she opened her laptop.

No story. Nothing from her editor demanding to know where her next chapter was. Only an email from Frank Merek expressing how upset he was that she'd chosen to quit, especially in this manner. Despite his disappointment, he wished her well, and Rachael closed her laptop with a satisfied smile.

Loading everything up took almost an hour since she insisted on resting between trips so as not to get all stinky. Once she had all of her essentials and some of her not-so-essentials in the vehicle, she placed Scrappy into her pet carrier and put her in a spot in the back where she'd be more comfortable. With one more glance around the apartment, she locked the door.

Graham had given her directions so that she could find Silverwood again, but there was no address, nothing to type into a GPS. When Rachael pulled out of the parking lot, it was only with a vague notion that she knew where to go. On the other hand, she'd created Silverwood, so surely she wouldn't have any trouble finding it now that it existed.

The two hour drive gave her plenty of chances to think about everything that had happened since she'd felt that small tremor while finishing the last chapter of her novel. She still had no idea what it was, but she couldn't help but feel as if it was connected somehow. Perhaps the library at Silverwood would have some clues as to what might've happened to bring her story to life. Though she had yet to see any magic at the school, she knew it was there, knew there were staff members and students who could do remarkable feats. Was it possible the school itself was also magical?

Rachael had never believed in magic. Driving along with the radio playing '90s music, she thought about how she'd always wished magic were real. As a little girl, she'd dreamt of waking up in a fairy tale and having powers that could bring her true happiness. She never quite understood why her father had left, but the idea that she could magically bring him back to her was an appealing one. As she got older, she realized she didn't want or need him back in her life. But magic still would've come in handy for other situations--like revenge. Or true love.

None of the magic at Silverwood worked that way. She couldn't learn a spell to make Graham fall in love with her. But she could learn to protect herself, and maybe how to use her mind to move things or set things on fire. That would be cool. Surely, in a world where that was possible, it was also a possibility that whatever had made her story come to life could be discovered at Silverwood.

After stopping for a bite to eat, Rachael found herself winding through the countryside a little before noon, hoping she could find the right road. She could hear Scrappy moving around in her carrier, growing anxious, or sensing the place where she could eventually find Graham not too far away. "We'll be there soon, kitty," she assured her furry friend. Some of the houses in the distance looked familiar, and she remembered the curve she was headed around now.

A few more miles, and she saw the trees up ahead, the ones that stood sentinel around the road where she would turn to reach Silver-wood. Rachael hit the brakes, turned on her blinker, and held her breath.

Awe overcame her, just as it had the day before when she was in Graham's Ferrari. The trees seemed mystical, with gnarled trunks and green leaves the summer sun had yet to fry to burnt brown. The meadows beyond the trees were also green, and Rachael could imagine deer and rabbits frolicking there. Concentrating on the road, she wound her way to the left and Silverwood came into view. Still there. Still part of her reality, despite how impossible it seemed.

To her left was a small keypad she hadn't seen the day before. She considered pushing the intercom button to ask to be buzzed in, but before she tried that, she entered the passcode Graham had set up for her for all of the doors to see if that would work here, too. The gates in front of her yawned open with a tired groan, and in front of her, Silverwood came to life.

21

GETTING SETTLED

Rachael

Ms. Post in the front office had been very helpful. By the time Rachael had finished checking in, she was confident all of the items remaining in her apartment would be packed and carefully placed in a storage unit on the academy property, her lease would be taken care of, and the secretary had even assigned her a parking spot in the garage for her car. With the lease she'd apparently taken out on the Infiniti being her only expense, Rachael felt confident she would be able to save a lot of money while she was in school at Silverwood. All of the positives of this experience were beginning to outweigh the negatives, like having the reality she'd known for over 25 years suddenly shift into something else.

The elevator doors opened on her floor, and Rachael pressed the button to keep the doors held open while she unpacked her second load of boxes from her car. She only had a few items left and didn't really need any help, though Tripp had yet to appear, and she hadn't bothered to text him. The roar of a box fan coming from Jazz's room made her think the girl was still sleeping.

Rachael moved the four boxes she'd brought up this time out into the hall and then released the elevator. "Hey, you need any help?"

She turned to see a younger guy with reddish brown hair and a sprinkle of freckles, his hands shoved deep into the pockets of his jeans. He looked like he was Jazz's age, maybe a year older at best, his long bangs hanging over one eye the way the kids were wearing it these days. "Oh, I think I can manage."

"I don't mind. I'm Rex. I live across the hall from Jazz--from you."

He didn't offer his hand, but Rachael did, figuring he was just too young to realize that was how introductions were properly made. "Rachael," she said, as he realized his mistake, shook his head, and gripped her offered hand. "Great to meet you." He smiled and let her hand go. "Okay, sure, if you're positive you don't mind."

"Not at all." He picked up one of her boxes, and Rachael grabbed another, walking down the hall as swiftly as she could. It wasn't heavy, but the wide girth made it a little awkward.

She'd propped her dorm room open for easier access. Scrappy meowed from her new prison cell--the bathroom, and Rex followed Rachael in, carefully setting the box down next to the ones from her last Tripp while Rachael more or less just dropped it. "Thanks."

"Sure thing." His smile was still timid, like he wasn't quite sure what to make of her. "Grab the others?"

"Yep."

They brought in the last two, and Rachael thought about what she had left in her car. Two suitcases and another bag she could sling over her shoulder. She should be able to get all of that in one trip by herself.

Rex seemed bored. "I really don't mind going down with you," he said as she explained she had one more load. "I've got nothing else to do."

"Cool." She wasn't going to argue with him if he wanted to help.

In the elevator, she considered trying to start a conversation, but he seemed like a person who didn't like to talk. The awkward silence got to her as they walked toward her car, which was pulled to the curb in the back of the building only a few steps away from the door that led to the freight elevator, the one she'd been using. "Where are you from, Rex?"

"Nebraska," he said, pulling Rachael's largest suitcase out of the back of her SUV. She went around to the passenger side and took out her smaller bag while he got the other suitcase out of the bag.

"That's everything," she told him, closing the back as she came around. The smaller suitcase was on rollers, so she took that one and let Rex carry the larger suitcase. "Thanks."

"Sure." That seemed to be his favorite word.

Back in the elevator, Rachael asked, "Nebraska, huh? You're a ways from home. Where abouts in Nebraska?"

"Hastings."

It was another one word answer. Rachael should've been deterred, but she wasn't. "Big city? Small town?"

"In-between. About twenty-five K."

Taking that to mean twenty-five thousand people, she nodded. "Not too bad. As long as there are things to do." The elevator opened and she led the way out.

"Yeah. A few things." Rex followed her down the hallway, a man of few words.

They reached her room and put her stuff down. She still had questions for him but knew she was going to have to pry answers out of him. "How long have you known about Silverwood?"

"My whole life. My dad works for 'em."

"Really? That's pretty cool. Did you just graduate from high school?"

"Yep."

She waited for him to say more, but when he didn't, Rachael surveyed the room, deciding it was time for Rex to go on his way so that she could unpack. "Well… thanks again."

"Yep."

"See you later." She smiled and gave him a little wave, and he backed toward the door with a "'K," and a few seconds later, she heard his door close.

Rachael couldn't help but smile. He was a sweet kid, but he was going to have to get over some of his awkwardness if he was going to be successful in an industry whose primary purpose was to pull the heads off monsters.

She'd just started unpacking, her door still propped and the meowing had stopped, when she heard footsteps in the hall. The contents of the box she was emptying had all of her attention until she heard a brisk knock on her open door.

Rachael turned her head to see another face she'd only seen in her own head before. Average height, with blond hair far lighter than a color that could've appeared natural, Tripp was a handsome fellow, especially when he smiled. His biceps bulged against his red button-down shirt, and the confident air that poured off him was opposite of Rex in every way possible.

"Hey, Rach!" he said, his hand extended as he crossed the threshold. "You made it!"

A smile instantly lit her face as she set down the photo album she'd just unpacked, placing it on the coffee table. "Hi. You must be Tripp."

"That's what I hear." His laugh was the sort of chuckle you might hear from a frat house late on a Friday night. Clasping her hand in both of his, he gave it a squeeze. "Great to have you here."

"Thanks. It's great to be here." He released her hand just short of pumping it free from her elbow.

"I woulda helped you move in." Tripp surveyed the boxes, hands on hips. "This everything?"

"It is." She looked around, too. She hadn't brought much with her. Not a lot of the items from her apartment were worth bringing along.

"You need any help unpacking?"

The idea of Tripp putting her panties in a drawer almost brought a blush to her face. "No, I'm good."

"All right. Well, Graham gave you my number, didn't he?" Rachael nodded. "Just give me a holler if you need anything. Looks like he'll be back sometime tomorrow."

Hoping her face didn't display her disappointment at hearing he wouldn't be back sooner, Rachael said, "Cool. Well, I'll just get unpacked and go put my car in the garage. Is it okay to sit by the elevator entrance a bit longer?"

"Sure, sure. No one else is moving in today, so it should be fine. You got your parking spot squared away with Ms. P.?"

"I did."

"Sweet." Tripp was just about to walk out the door when a second set of footsteps echoed down the hallway. Rachael hoped it was one of the trainers or professors, someone she was excited to meet, but when the form of a petite woman with a scowl on her pretty face filled the doorway, she inhaled sharply and tried not to cringe. "Oh, hey, Sammi."

Sammi Knight stepped into Rachael's room, the scowl somehow deepening. "This is your room?"

It was evident to Rachael why Chell's sister would ask such a question, but she wasn't supposed to know this had been Chell's room when she first moved into Silverwood, so she had to pretend to be confused. "Yes. Hi, I'm Rachael." She offered her hand.

Sammi was still looking around, her arms folded, but when she realized Rachael had her hand extended, she looked at it, and with a heavy sigh, shook it quickly, yet firmly. "Graham let you pick this room?"

"Yes…. Is there a problem?" Rachael wondered how much she was willing to say.

An internal argument delayed the answer as Sammi's eyes darted back and forth in consideration. Eventually, she shrugged and said, "No. Just… surprised."

"Sammi, Rachael's grandfather was one of us. Graham's very excited about her potential."

Tripp's statement would've made Rachael feel flattered if it wasn't for Sammi's response. Her face crinkled again as she stared at him. "Awesome." She looked around the room one more time. "Nice to meet you, Rach. See you around." The trainer was gone as quickly as she'd appeared.

Rachael stood dumbfounded for a moment, trying to figure out whether or not she should respond.

"Don't... worry about her." Tripp took a few steps closer, keeping his voice low. "She's not herself right now. Her sister passed away recently."

"Oh." Rachael didn't know what else to say. "I'm sorry to hear that."

"Yeah. It was terrible for all of us, but especially Sammi--and Graham. She was his fiancée."

Rachael tried to make a surprised face as if she hadn't put two and two together. "I see."

"So... she might need some time. I think this room might've been Sammi's sister's at one point."

Rachael was getting good at looking shocked. "If I'd known that...."

"No, it's fine." Tripp was standing next to her now and he gently put his hand on her shoulder. Rachael wasn't sure what to make of that. "She'll just need some time. She'll come around. You seem like a cool person, and I haven't heard Graham so excited about a new recruit in a while, so I'm sure Sammi will be fine, once she gets to know you." He pulled his hand back and put it in his pocket.

"I hope so." Rachael smiled at him, but she knew there wasn't much of a chance of that. Sammi must somehow sense that Rachael was the one responsible for her sister's death. Even though there couldn't possibly be any evidence of that in this world, she knew, deep inside herself. Rachael wasn't ever going to be able to win Sammi Knight over. Hopefully, she could keep her from discovering her hunch was right, or who knew what she might do to Rachael. It wouldn't be pretty.

22

AN AWFUL DISCOVERY

Rachael

THE FOOD in the cafeteria wasn't half bad. In fact, Rachael was impressed with her own work when it came to creating chefs and other staff who were willing to work at this secret facility when they could've been working at gourmet restaurants by the taste of the cuisine. Not that she'd put anything too fancy on her plate when she had made her selections, but the pizza and garlic bread was much better than any of the local places near her apartment in Baltimore, and the fettuccini alfredo Rex had in front of him looked pretty darn good, too.

It took Jazz a few minutes to join them. She was chatting with some guy, a student Rachael hadn't met yet. He was kind of cute, but definitely way too young for her--probably Jazz's age. He had dark hair and looked like he probably lifted twice a day all the way through high school and beyond.

When Jazz finally found her way to the table, the uncomfortable silence that had settled around them was instantly lifted. "Sorry guys, but he was just too cute not to chat up." She looked over her shoulder with a smile, watching the boy take a seat at a fairly crowded table next to a blonde girl and a redheaded boy. All of them had to have been fairly new recruits, they were so young. It didn't seem to deter Jazz that he was sitting next to a pretty girl.

"No problem," Rachael said with a smile, biting into her pizza. She finished chewing before she asked, "Do you know him?"

"I know his name is Jorge, and he's a Lower Spring. I think there are only ten people in that group. I guess it's hard to get recruits in the spring semester. I've talked to him a few times, but usually that blonde girl, Claira, is around."

"Is that his girlfriend?" Rachael asked, taking a sip of her soda. She didn't remember inventing any of these people.

"I don't know," Jazz said with a shrug. She took a big bite of lasagna, so Rachael had a feeling she wouldn't be saying more for a while.

"She's not," Rex said, twirling his fork through his pasta. "I think she'd like to be, but they're not a couple."

"How do you know that?" Jazz was still chewing, but at least her mouth was mostly empty.

"Just do." He smiled at her slightly and shrugged, and as Jasmine started talking about how cute Jorge was, Rex pulled his phone out of his pocket. Rachael couldn't blame him for not wanting to listen to his neighbor talk about how cute another guy was. Rex wasn't bad looking, but Jazz seemed to like guys who were more outgoing.

Jazz was in the middle of a story about some guy from her high school that all the girls liked. In her opinion, he looked a lot like Jorge but not as hot, when Rex made a low humming noise and whispered, "Oh, shit."

It was enough to make Jazz stop talking mid-sentence, which was saying a lot. "What is it, Rex? What are you watching?"

"I was just scrolling through social media, but a video popped up that a friend of mine from high school tagged me in because he knows I moved out this way. Apparently, a family was slaughtered last night in a suburb of Baltimore. He was just telling me to be careful, but... when I looked at the video... I have a feeling this might be something more than just a homicide."

"Can we see?" Jazz asked, scooting around the table so that she was sitting at Rex's elbow before he even answered. He leaned away from her for a moment, clearly uncomfortable, so Rachael decided to walk around to the back of his chair to watch, rather than sandwich him between two women.

Rachael watched the news report and didn't notice anything unusual until the very end when the cameraman panned across the exterior of the house. Next to one of the windows in the front of the house, there appeared to be something etched into the wood. If Rachael hadn't been looking carefully, she would've missed it. How Rex even knew to look for it was unbeknownst to her. He backed the video up slightly and froze it right in the exact spot she needed to see. "Is that an S with a slash through it?"

"Yeah," Rex said. "Not good."

Rachael remembered that Rex's family had been in this line of work for a while, so that must be how he knew what the symbol meant. Jazz just looked confused. "So?" she asked, leaning in closer to the phone.

"So... that's the mark Sasha Thornsby leaves when she attacks," Rex replied. "She must've left it on the outside of the house to make sure we saw it, even if we didn't know she was back."

Rachael sunk into her chair, pushing her tray out of the way. Her appetite was gone. Sasha Thornsby was the most violent, most powerful vampire ever to walk the face of the earth. She'd been Chell's arch-nemesis for years, and they'd battled in some of the craziest places--on the ledges of rooftops, mountainsides, even under water. Chell had eventually figured out a spell that had locked Sasha in a cavern beneath a glacier in Greenland late last year, but now that Chell was gone, the spell must've been broken.

It hadn't occurred to Rachael that killing Chell would free Sasha. In fact, she hadn't intended to write it that way at all. She was going to have Sasha get free eventually, once Rachael figured out who her new protagonist was, and had her thoroughly trained and ready to fight. Now, however, Sasha was back, and Rachael had no control over what was happening with anyone, not even herself.

By the time Rachael had tuned back in, Rex was halfway through explaining how awful Sasha was and how she was responsible for killing hundreds of people, as well as turning dozens more. "She's been gone for a few months," Rex said, "but it definitely seems like she's back now."

"And she leaves that mark whenever she kills someone?" Jazz asked.

"Yeah. It's usually more difficult to find, but in this case, I think she wants us to know," Rex was saying.

"Huh." Jazz scooted back around in front of her food and started eating again while Rachael tried not to stare at her, or anyone, but it was hard because she wasn't sure what to think about any of this. After all, it was sort of her fault that the worst vampire in creation had suddenly been released into the world--and this time she had no idea how to stop her.

23

UNEXPECTED

Rachael

BACK IN HER DORM ROOM, Rachael had her laptop open. Scrappy snuggled up next to her leg while she looked through report after report noting the violent actions of one Sasha Thornsby. Even though Rachael had written several of the scenes noted in the reports herself, she wanted to go through as many as she possibly could, especially the ones she wasn't aware of for whatever reason. Sasha had been around for hundreds of years, so there were plenty that predated the antagonistic relationship between the bloodsucker and Chell. The ones from before the hunter entered her life were foreign to Rachael, as were Sasha's activities in other parts of the world.

She'd accessed a database she wasn't supposed to even know existed yet. It wasn't something students were ever made aware of, not unless they were asked to join the team. If that happened at all, it wouldn't be until after she finished her two year program. So Rachael should've had no idea the VRD, or Vampire Reports Database, for lack of a cooler sounding name, even existed, let alone known how to get in without being granted credentials or her own password. She was using Chell's, which had never been deactivated. If anyone happened to check the logs in the next few days to see who had been snooping around, they might get a little bit of a shock, but she doubted anyone would be paying too close attention to the login history.

Sasha was a beast. Page after page of detailed accounts of her murderous rampages read like a series of horror movies. Rachael had purposely crafted the woman to be a badass, nearly unstoppable, so that Chell would have to be all the stronger for taking her out. Of course, if Rachael had realized at the time she'd actually be the one who'd have to find a way to destroy the vampire once and for all, she might've written in an Achilles heel. Since there didn't seem to be one, she hoped information from the reports might be useful. So far, all it was doing was making her stomach roll and her head hurt.

At least her bed was comfortable. After she'd gotten completely unpacked, she'd realized her bed at home had a full-sized mattress, and this was a queen, so she'd had to go into town to buy some new linens. Imagine her surprise when she saw the exact same comforter set that Chell had purchased two years ago still on the shelf in her local discount department store. The red and gold really did look nice with the beige walls of the bedroom, and the fabric was a lot softer than Rachael had realized. Scrappy was comfortable, anyway, and that meant something. She wished she could put her computer down and get some rest herself, but she had a feeling the moment she closed her eyes, nightmares where Sasha ripped her throat out would invade her every thought.

It was getting late. The clock on her nightstand said it was past midnight, and she could hear Jazz's box fan whirring through the wall, though it wasn't as loud in her bedroom as it had been when she'd heard it from the hallway earlier. The idea that she should quit reading about drained bodies and terrorized teens crossed her mind again. She could go to the library tomorrow and see if there was anything helpful in there. That had been where Chell had discovered the spell that had locked Sasha in that cave. There might be other useful incantations to be had. Perhaps she could go back to the original manuscript notes she still had on her laptop, the earliest version, and plug some magic words in. Would that work?

A light knock on her door had her pausing mid-solution. Who would be stopping by this time of night? She figured it had to be Rex. He had seemed just as concerned about Sasha as Rachael was earlier. She set her laptop aside and went to the door, glad she was still somewhat presentable in a nice pair of pajamas she'd picked up at the store. Not only were the adorable bunnies hard to pass up, she realized she couldn't let any more of her teammates catch her looking a mess the way Graham had.

Her planning paid off when she pulled the door open to see familiar lavender eyes. "Graham?" Her voice was a squeaky whisper. "What are you doing here?"

"Sorry. I didn't wake you did I?"

Realizing her surprise may have sounded unwelcoming, Rachael shook her head and found a smile. "No, not at all. I thought… you weren't coming back until tomorrow."

"I wasn't." He shifted his weight from one black boot to the other. "I have to leave again in the morning, in a few hours. I just… wanted to see if you got settled okay."

A glint in his eyes told her this was more than just checking up on a new recruit, though she couldn't quite identify what it was about his tone, the way he was looking at her, that let her know that was the case. Rachael felt her heart pound inside of her chest as she weighed the options. "I did, thanks," she muttered, leaning against the door and trying to decide whether or not she should ask him in. Why was he really here?

"Good. Did Tripp help you with the boxes?"

"Nah, I got Rex to help me. He's a good kid."

Graham chuckled, running a hand through those luscious locks. "Yeah, he is a good kid. He's not that much younger than you, Rach."

She shrugged. "I'm old enough to be these kids'… older sister. Or aunt." She wasn't old enough to be their mom, even if it seemed like it.

He shook his head at her but didn't further comment. Scrappy suddenly sprang to life behind her, realizing who was at the door, and shot past the partially open divide between the living room and bedroom, on Graham's leg before even the lightning fast vampire hunter could react. "Well, hello there, kitty."

"Sorry." Rachael had gotten the impression he wasn't a huge fan of cats, but he wasn't backing away now like he had the other day at her apartment. "She just really loves you."

He bent down to pet her, and Scrappy's purring filled the hall. "It's okay. She's sweet." He stood, and Scrappy laid down on the floor at his feet, still tired from her exhausting day of catnapping.

Again, as lavender met blue, she pondered whether she should ask him in. She hadn't even asked about his trip or where he was headed the next day. Or why he was here....

"I should probably let you get some sleep. I'm sure it's been a long day for you."

"Oh, yeah. Well, okay." Sentences, Rachael, she scolded herself. "I mean... I was just surfing the Internet. Did you...." she paused, watching his face for an indication that he knew what she was going to ask and how he might respond. His eyebrows arched, but he didn't do her the service of jumping in and finishing the sentence. "Did you get your recruit?" On the inside, she groaned, thinking she probably sounded as stupid to him as she did to herself.

"I did. His name is Tony. He's a little older than the other two kids, twenty-two. He'll be here next week."

"Great." She wondered what Tony would be like, but she couldn't pull her eyes away from the man in front of her to try to picture him. Graham was wearing his leather jacket, and though he looked tired, his five o'clock shadow long passed into something closer to a fifteen year old's first attempt at a beard, thoughts of grabbing his collar and tugging him into her room came to mind, and she had to fight them off to hear what he was saying.

"I should be back to campus tomorrow afternoon. Feel free to wander around tomorrow. Visit the library, go watch the training in the gym, that sort of thing. You can use the workout room, too, if you want to. You should have your first semester schedule tomorrow or the next day, and Tripp will probably stop by tomorrow with your badge and any access codes you didn't get today."

"Awesome." She wished she could think of something better to say, but visions of pressing herself against him, of sinking her teeth into that bottom lip, were messing with her head.

He shifted again; she knew he was going to walk away, and she wouldn't see him again until tomorrow afternoon at best. While she wanted him to stay, she had to remember this wasn't just a book to him. He had just lost a very real fiancée, and it was way too soon for him to be considering starting anything up.

So… why was he there?

"Have a good night, Rach."

"Thanks. You too. Thank you for stopping by."

Graham smiled at her, holding her gaze for a second, and then headed off down the hallway. Scrappy stood, watching him with longing in her eyes, and Rachael focused on her cat, not his retreating form, though her heart concurred with her kitty. "Come on, Scrap. Let's get some sleep."

Reluctantly, Scrappy headed inside of the dorm room, and Rachael locked the door, flicking off the main light switch as she headed back to her bedroom. Exactly why Graham had shown up, she might not ever know. But the fact that he had done so left a smile on her face.

She didn't put her laptop away just yet, though. Instead, she logged out of VRD and searched for, "How long after a girlfriend dies can I make my move?"

2 4

A SEARCH

Rachael

DREAMS OF GRAHAM were not that uncommon for Rachael. In fact, over the years, she had probably dreamt of the man with the lavender eyes more often than she'd dreamt of anyone else. However, now that she'd met him in person, and he wasn't just a figment of her imagination, waking up to the realization that she'd had a vivid dream about him, and not the kind one shared openly with their mother, made her a little nervous to see him later in the day. What if he could read it all over her face?

Trying not to think about it, Rachael focused on Sasha and her plan to go to the library to see if she could find another spell that might work against the vampire. Taking a shower in her new bathroom also got her mind off things--until she remembered a particularly steamy shower Chell had taken in this same bathroom, not alone--and had to rush to get the shampoo out of her hair and turn the water to cold for a few seconds. Perhaps choosing Chell's room wasn't a good idea after all....

Dressed in jeans and a nice T-shirt with a cardigan over top in case the AC was chilly, Rachael made sure her makeup was on point and then slipped on some comfortable sneakers. She planned to swing by the cafe for breakfast on her way to the library, but she knew Jazz wouldn't be joining her as the fan was still whirring; it wasn't 9:00 yet, which meant her next door neighbor likely wouldn't be up for at least another two hours. Deciding to stop by Rex's room on the way downstairs, she grabbed her laptop, shoved it in a back-pack, picked up a notebook and a pen, and slipped that inside, too.

In the hall, she could hear footsteps and voices coming from one of the adjoining walkways, but no one was out and about in their section of the dorm, probably because the students from Upper Summer were already in class or in the gym. Rachael knocked on Rex's door and waited a few moments. He didn't answer, so she figured he might already be in the cafe or had gone to the gym. Making a mental note to get his phone number so she could text him next time, she headed for the stairs.

She'd reached the first landing when she heard someone coming her way. The steps were light and even, like a small determined person. Rachael's stomach twisted in a knot, and she said a little prayer that it would be anyone except the person she dreaded seeing, but when she rounded the corner to go down the next half-flight of steps, she met Sammi Knight's eyes.

"Good morning." Rachael forced a smile, reminding herself Sammi had no reason to dislike her--as far as the trainer knew. "How are you?"

"Fine." Sammi's smile was a thin line that showed no teeth. She looked at Rachael's bag and then back at her face. "You haven't started class yet, have you?"

"No, no, not until the first. I just thought I'd check out the library."

Sammi nodded, but her expression showed she hadn't accepted that answer. She seemed suspicious. Without another word, Sammi hurried past her, and Rachael turned to watch her go for a few seconds before she quietly said, "See ya later."

"Yep," Sammi called without turning around.

Rachael moved on, feeling dissed by her own character. Sure, she was used to them doing their own thing and ignoring her while she was writing, but she never would've expected one of them to be so rude, right to her face.

At least Rex was in the cafeteria when she got there, which meant she wouldn't have to sit alone. He had a stack of pancakes in front of him so he wouldn't be finishing any time soon. It wasn't hard for her to find her smile again, despite Sammi's attitude, when he looked up and acknowledged her with a grin. Letting her bag slide down her arm to her hand, Rachael made her way to the table. "Hey, good morning. Can I join you?" She slung her bag over the back of the chair before he even answered.

"Please, have a seat," Rex said, more comfortable with her on day two than he had been the day before. "Jazz still sleeping?"

"Fan's still on, so I'm thinking yes." She chuckled and headed off to grab some pancakes and juice, noting there were only a few other students in the cafeteria at the moment. Getting up early for classes that started at 8:00 might be a bit of a struggle. While she was used to fairly early mornings, she wasn't used to making herself presentable before noon, not since she'd quit Merek and Merek. She figured she'd get used to it again. Eventually.

Rex was reading something on his phone when Rachael got back to the table, the forkful of pancake he had poised over his plate dripping syrup as he focused on the words and not the food. "Rex? You okay?" She pulled out the chair next to him, and the screeching sound of the metal legs on the tile brought him out of his stupor.

"Oh, yeah. Fine." He blinked a few times and then remembered he was mid-bite. He placed the soggy pancakes in his mouth and set his phone down.

Rachael cut her pancakes up while she asked, "Did you find something else out about Sasha?" She kept her voice down, even though the other students in the cafe were several tables away and were not paying any attention to them.

Still chewing, Rex nodded, and Rachael felt the hairs on her arms stand on end. After he swallowed, he said, "I think she might be responsible for another slaughter in New York state. I have a feeling she was working her way back here from wherever she was."

She took a deep breath and a few bites of her breakfast while she pondered his statement. Washing it down with a drink of her juice, she considered whether or not they should continue down this path or let someone else handle it. "Do you think they know?" she asked, assuming he'd know she was talking about the hunters and others in charge of the academy.

Shaking his head, Rex put his empty fork down on his plate, clearly done with his breakfast. "I don't think they've had a chance to look at it yet. Graham's out of town. Tripp has been working on local recruits. I think he's headed back out today. The trainers and professors are all working, and there doesn't seem to be anything suspicious reported in the news. Nothing that indicates it's Sasha anyway. They may think it's a vampire, but if they don't realize it's her, they probably won't act quickly. Or they'll let locals handle it, and that's probably not the best idea."

"Because they're not strong enough to take her out?"

"Precisely."

"But then... who is?"

Rex shook his head again. "Without Chell Knight here, I don't know."

Rachael looked at her plate again. She hadn't taken too many bites, but she was also not hungry anymore. As far as Rex knew, Rachael wouldn't have a clue who Chell was, but she couldn't get her face to cooperate well enough to fool him so that he'd feel obligated to explain. He'd just have to assume she'd heard things--which she had--but nothing about how powerful a hunter Chell had been. "We'll just have to figure something out, I guess," she concluded, not sure what that something might be.

Scooting his chair back, Rex grabbed hold of his tray. "I think I'm going to go see if I can track down Tripp before he leaves. He should know. Sorry to leave you to eat alone."

"That's okay. I've kind of lost my appetite."

Rex's smile was empathetic as he crossed the cafeteria to turn in his tray. Tripp was supposed to give Rachael her badge, amongst other things that day, and since he hadn't done that yet, she thought maybe Rex could find him before he left campus. Hopefully, Tripp would take Rex seriously and not blow this off. It seemed like Sasha had come to Chell's back yard on purpose, and whatever it was the vampire was looking for, someone would have to stop her. The body count was piling up, and Rachael didn't want to be responsible for any more innocent lives being lost. If only there was a way to bring Chell back. Even if that would mean she'd lose her chance with Graham, that would be better than Sasha running free, wouldn't it?

Realizing it didn't matter because Chell wasn't coming back, Rachael followed Rex's trail to turn in her dishes, determined to get to the library and see what she could find. If Chell was clever enough to find a way to lock Sasha up, Rachael had to be, too, because she'd created Chell in the first place. She only hoped the world she'd created had a magic strong enough to incarcerate the vampire again, and hopefully, for good this time, because she doubted any of them were capable of destroying Sasha Thornsby.

25

PROF. MCCALL

Rachael

THE HALLS WERE ESSENTIALLY empty as Rachael made her way from the cafeteria into the academic building on her way to the library. She realized there was more than one way to get there but had ended up using the entrance closest to the gym. The sounds of the trainers encouraging their students caught her attention, and she was tempted to peek her head inside. She remembered Graham saying she could watch if she wanted to. But then, she was afraid Sammi might be in there, and she didn't want to see the other woman at the moment, if she could avoid it. So she kept walking, heading away from the gym toward one of the academic wings, the one where the history classes were taught.

Many of the classrooms were empty, and Rachael realized she'd made the hallways far too long for the amount of students that attended Silverwood, particularly since they weren't required to take very many classes. She made a mental note to change that should she ever find herself writing another academy series. The idea of writing anything at all was terrifying considering she could apparently bring whatever she constructed to real life somehow. She doubted she'd be writing anything any time soon.

Lost in her own thoughts, Rachael realized she'd missed the turn-off she'd been looking for that led to the library. She could keep going straight, toward the painting of Graham Silverwood, and then take a different hallway, but she'd intended to use the one that joined to the hall she was standing in, just before Professor McCall's classroom.

She turned around and headed the few steps back, thinking it was strange she hadn't met Dr. McCall yet when his classroom door opened to her left and the instructor came out. He was wiping his cheeks, his head downcast, and he didn't notice her at first. The only reason she knew for certain it was him was because his name was on the plate outside of the classroom, and she recognized his haircut. His short, light brown hair was meticulously parted on the side and looked like what one would expect from a college professor, except for the cowlick in the front which he had embraced long ago and kept styled at an odd angle with enough product that it never seemed to move, not even now as he stood outside of his busy classroom, sobbing.

Rachael froze, not sure what she should do. He was obviously upset and lost in his own thoughts, and she didn't want to interrupt, but she also felt responsible and wanted to see if he was okay. She took a few more steps, timidly, and when he looked up and saw her looking at him, pink crept into his cheeks. He swiped at his tears as if he were a small child trying to hide any evidence of spoiling his dinner with cookies. "Uh, hi." He cleared his throat. "Can I help you with something?"

A wave of nausea washed over Rachael and her forehead crinkled as uncomfortable thoughts filled her head. Deja vu. She was having deja vu. "Oh, no, I'm… I was just looking for the library." She pointed down the hallway up ahead of her and to the right, indicating that she knew now where she was headed. She wasn't lost. She wasn't a new, lost student that he needed to help--before rushing back in to continue the lesson he'd been instructing his students on the importance of being completely prepared when entering a fray with a bloodsucker.

"The library is right up that hallway." Jared smiled at her, his tears dried up, only a few trails marking his face now. He was handsome in an unassuming way. Rachael tried not to stare at him, but the sensation of seeing someone she'd dreamt up face-to-face was still an oddity to her, though she should've been getting used to it by now. "You can't miss it."

"Thank you," Rachael said, knowing she shouldn't have been able to miss it the first time she walked past the hallway. "I appreciate it, Professor McCall."

"Sure." His forehead furrowed. "How did you know my name?"

Rachael cleared her throat. At least this time, she had a reasonable explanation for having information she shouldn't have access to yet. "The nameplate–by your classroom door."

Jared turned and looked over his shoulder at the wall before he nodded. "Right." For some reason, she got the impression he wasn't buying that explanation. Why, she had no idea. It wasn't as if she couldn't read. Wouldn't most people have reached the same conclusion she did? A gentleman steps out of a classroom wearing a brown suit and tie, his hair is nicely arranged, and he's old enough to be a professor--a newish one anyway. It seemed pretty obvious to her that most people would've made the same assumption she was claiming to have made.

Except, that wasn't how she knew this was Jared McCall. She knew this was Jared McCall because she'd created him herself.

"I'm afraid I didn't catch your name," Dr. McCall said, his grayish-blue eyes narrowing in on her.

With a deep breath, she said, "Rachael. I'm Rachael."

"It's nice to meet you, Rachael," Dr. McCall was saying, but Rachael was having difficulty listening to him as the floor beneath her feet shifted slightly, a minor tremble compared to the last time she'd felt the earth quake.

Her eyes wide, she looked up at him and noticed he was staring at her with that questioning expression on his face again. "Is everything all right?"

"Did you… did you feel that?"

"Feel what?"

He hadn't. The earth hadn't moved at all for him. Rachael took another deep breath, and deciding she shouldn't be the "new freak girl," she looked around and saw a vent in the ceiling nearby. "Oh, I guess the AC just kicked on." She laughed like she'd been referring to a strong breeze and not the earth moving on its axis in an erratic, jarring sensation. "Thanks again, Professor." She needed to get away from him as soon as humanly possible.

"Sure thing, Rachael. See you around."

Rachael gave him a wave and headed off down the hall that led to the library, but she felt his eyes on the back of her until she had rounded the corner out of his sight. Jared McCall seemed to suspect something was out of the ordinary, whether he'd felt the earth move or not. Rachael hoped she could make him an ally because he was the most intelligent individual on campus, and if anyone could help her figure out what was going on, it was him. Having him working against her would be almost as dangerous as having Sammi Knight hate her, and since Chell's sister already seemed to want to kill her, Rachael needed someone on her side, someone like Jared McCall.

2 6

THE LIBRARY

Rachael

THE LIBRARY WAS GINORMOUS, and as Rachael stood just inside the doorway, looking up at rows and rows of books, across to even more books on the other side of the circular space, she had to wonder what in the world she'd been thinking when she created such an expansive area that played such a small part in the plot of her story. Perhaps it had been because she loved books so much herself or that she'd been inspired by the dramatic visuals of seeing thousands of books all at once in some of her favorite movies--like *Beauty and the Beast*. Maybe it just felt right to have such a place in any school. Standing there before it all, she wondered if there were even words on the pages of all of these books. Where had they come from? When she'd somehow brought the world from her own books to life, had the authors who allegedly scribed these bound volumes also come with them? She had to imagine that was the case, but none of it made any sense to her.

Fumbling for the light switch by the door, Rachael filled the room with light. The soft glow from the skylight in the domed ceiling had only reached the open center of the room. Now, the bookshelves looked even more impressive. She could see them all clearly with the lights on. Her stomach tightened as she realized she had no idea where to start. With a deep breath, Rachael walked into the room and let her fingers run along the spines, realizing there were more books here than she could possibly read in two lifetimes.

A librarian would've been helpful. Unfortunately, when Ms. Turner had retired a few months ago, right after Chell banished Sasha to the cave, Rachael hadn't seen fit to replace her. There'd been no need. Thus, the lights had been off, the shelves were slightly dusty, and the scent of millions of pages of paper had taken over what would've smelled like a special cinnamon potpourri Ms. Turner made herself and kept freshly strewn in small baskets around the library to keep the room "crisp and fresh."

"I could sure use your help right now, Page Turner," Rachael muttered. The name sounded even sillier than her other characters' names when spoken aloud, but she didn't take the time to laugh. Instead, she stood and surveyed the room, trying to remember if she'd given a description of where Chell had found the book that had allowed her to lock Sasha away the first time. Had she written the title in her novel? Surely, she had. She'd just have to remember what it was.

Rachael's eyes wandered over section labels. This library didn't have the usual Dewey Decimal System since almost all of the books were on the same few topics--the history of vampires and vampire hunters, and of course, magic. She saw plenty of interesting labels, many of which might be useful, but she didn't know where to begin. Would "Spells Against the Undead" be a good place, or "Unusual Historical Weapons"? What about "Hidden Spaces and Portals" or "Rare Locks and Keys"? There was just so much in front of her, it was difficult to decide what to look at first.

Finally making a decision, Rachael headed over to the section containing books with spells she could potentially cast against Sasha, once she knew how to use her magic, and looked through the titles. Several seemed interesting, so she pulled them off the shelf and headed to one of the reading nooks Ms. Turner had created so that all of her students and staff members could be "cozy and comfortable" while reading. Setting the stack down on a table next to a couch, she sank into the cushion, a tiny bit of dust coming out of the fabric as she did so, and absently wondered if it was too late to get Ms. Turner back.

Flipping through the table of contents of the first book, Rachael saw a few chapters that looked like they could help, so she began to scan them, reading some more carefully than others. She had gotten through three books in such fashion when she realized her phone was vibrating, so she pulled it out of her pocket, setting the book aside. It was Tripp. With a sigh, she glanced at the stack of books, wishing she'd had more luck, and answered. "Hello?"

"Hey, Rach! It's Tripp. How's it going?"

He sounded far too chipper for someone who fought vampires for a living. Perhaps he still didn't realize Sasha was back. Maybe Rex hadn't been able to reach him yet. "I'm good, Tripp. How are you?" Rachael managed, not really feeling it at all.

"Good, good. Say, I was just about to head out to meet with a new recruit, but I wanted to get you your badge and a few other things first. Can I swing by and drop them off before I go?"

"Sure--but I'm not in my room right now. I'm in the library."

"Perfect! I'm right down the hall. I'll be there in a couple of minutes."

"Cool," Rachael said, but she realized the books she'd selected earlier might seem a little suspicious to Tripp. Her subject matter didn't quite seem to fit with something a new student would want to read about. She'd have to hurry to get them back on the shelf before he got there and started asking questions. "See you in a bit."

"See ya, Ra--" was all he got out before she hung up and popped up off the couch, grabbing the stack of books as she went.

Rachael had no idea where each specific book had come from, except for the section, and without a librarian, there was a good chance they'd never be put back correctly. She hurriedly shoved them into empty slots on the shelves where she'd been earlier and had just gotten the last one pushed into place when the library door opened.

As fast as she could go, she darted to another section of the library and grabbed a book off the shelf, pretending she was nonchalantly browsing and not looking for anything specific. At least she wouldn't pique his curiosity about her interest in spells since this book was on a different subject.

"Hey, Rach!" Tripp exclaimed, making short work of the distance between them. "Nice to see you."

"Nice to see you, too." She closed the book and leaned against the shelf, resting leisurely. She wasn't up to anything. Just hanging out....

"This is a pretty awesome space, isn't it?"

"Yeah, yeah. It's great." She looked around, nodding.

"Too bad we haven't gotten a new librarian yet. Ms. Turner is just about impossible to replace."

"Indeed." Rachael realized that sounded stupid coming out of her mouth but wasn't sure what more to say.

"Anywho… I gotta split, but here's your badge and a few other items you might need." He handed over a lanyard with a badge attached to it. The picture was one Ms. Post had taken of Rachael when she'd arrived the day before. It wasn't a bad shot, if she did say so herself. The rest were papers with information such as the pass-words she'd need to access certain websites and her schedule. "We don't require you to wear the badge all the time, but you should have it with you."

"Got it. Thank you." She smiled at him, piling the papers on top of the book she'd been flipping through.

"If you need anything before Graham or I get back, just go to the office or give Ms. Post a ring. She'll be able to help you."

"Awesome."

"All right, Rach. See you later." He smiled again, gave her a little wave, and then backed up a few steps before turning and walking out of the library without seeming to even acknowledge what section she'd been perusing, which was a good thing because Rachael had no idea where she was standing and would've had no explanation for the book if he'd asked.

Her bag was back by the couch, so she slid the paperwork and her badge off on an empty part of the shelf so she could put the book away. She caught a glimpse of the title as she put it back where she'd found it. <u>Collision of Worlds </u>by Dr. Wadsworth J. McCall. Rachael wondered if the writer was any relation to Jared but didn't otherwise pay it much mind as she grabbed her stuff and headed back to her bag. She'd had enough library exploration for one day. Deciding she'd go back online for a while before lunch, she made sure she had everything and took off, hoping her next visit to the library would be fruitful. This trip had yielded nothing important--nothing at all.

27

WHO WAS SHE?

Jared

JARED MCCALL WENT BACK into his classroom, glad to see his students still discussing the topic he'd left them with when he'd ran out of the room a few moments ago. It was funny how grief could sneak up on him. He never would've thought a topic as broad as preparation before a fray could trigger such deep emotions in him, but just the mention of a specific battle he'd fought with Chell had him weeping like a small child. If any of his students noticed, they said nothing, though a few had sympathetic looks on their faces now as he walked back to his desk.

Jared managed to get himself together enough to move on to the next part of his lecture, but his mind kept going back to the new student he'd met in the hallway. She'd said her name was Rachael, but he hadn't been thinking logically enough to ask her last name. There was something different about her. If Graham had mentioned her, Jared couldn't remember it. They hadn't talked as much lately as they usually did. Seeing Graham just reminded him that Chell was gone, and he didn't want to look for reminders if he could help it. Whatever it was about Rachael that had sparked a question in his mind, Jared couldn't shake it, and by the time the class period was over, he was curious enough to seek out more information about the brunette.

As the students filed out of his classroom, he reminded them that they'd be taking their final the next day and then quickly prepared for his next class. He had an hour off before the next set of students came in, which should be enough time to do a little bit of research. He didn't think Graham was on campus at the moment. If he recalled correctly, he was out on a recruiting trip. With the next semester starting soon, the recruiters would be very busy trying to get all of the students enrolled before classes started on Monday.

Jared stepped out into the hallway. His footsteps echoed off the tile in the emptiness; all the students had moved on to their next classes or to lunch. He had always wondered why the building was so large when the student body was never more than a few hundred at best. Perhaps Graham Silverwood had envisioned larger enrollment numbers when he'd dreamt up the academy so many decades ago.

Deciding to go to the office to see if he could find Rachael's file, Jared took a few steps that direction, but then a familiar cadence of footsteps caught his attention, and he turned to see Tripp coming up the hall, heading from the direction of the library. Since that's where Rachael had been going, Jared decided to try his luck with Tripp.

"Hey, Dr. M. How's it going?" Tripp asked, his carefree attitude coming through in his tone and swagger.

"Good, good," Jared said, smiling and stopping a few steps in front of Tripp, who seemed to be in a hurry. "Did you just come from the library?"

"Sure did. Had to deliver some paperwork before I head out for another recruitment meeting. Man, the kids are tough this time around. At this rate, we might not even have ten people in this class."

"Really?" That was surprising to Jared. The summer class was always the smallest, but he couldn't remember the last time they had less than a dozen students.

"Yeah. I'm not sure what's going on. It's like... no one's telling these kids about their lineage anymore. Most of them have no idea vampires even exist. Weird."

"That is weird," Jared agreed, mostly just because he didn't want to stay on that topic. "Say, was Rachael in the library when you were there?"

"Rachael? Yeah, she was in there. That's whose stuff I was delivering. You met her then? Now, there's a student that shows promise."

Glad Tripp was familiar with her, Jared nodded. "Did you recruit her?"

"Nah, Graham did. It was weird, too. She just suddenly showed up on our reports earlier this week. It was so odd. Her grandfather was a hunter, though, so she definitely belongs here. Just can't understand why we'd never seen her name on any of our lists before, especially not back when she was graduating from high school. I went back and checked, and nothing." He was shaking his head, his hands on his hips.

Jared thought it was strange, too, but he was more interested in what they did know about Rachael than what they didn't know. "Who was her grandfather?"

"Wessley Barnes," Tripp said confidently. "Did you know him? I think he retired before I started school here."

Shaking his head, Jared said, "No, I didn't know him either. But I have heard of him. So... it's Rachael Barnes?"

"Yep, that's her. Is everything okay?"

Jared realized he was stroking his chin and probably had a contemplative expression on his face. "Oh, yeah, everything's fine. I ran into her earlier. She seems like a nice woman. I just thought there was something... familiar about her. That's all." Jared didn't want to tell him it wasn't familiarity--it was an oddness, something about the way she'd looked at him, the way she'd known his name despite the fact that Jared had never noticed her looking at the nameplate on the wall.

"Well, she's definitely nice. A little older than the other new students, but I think that's cool. She's got a lot of potential."

Nodding, Jared said, "That's good," not sure what else to say. "I don't want to keep you."

"Thanks. I've gotta head out now. Nice talkin' to you, Doc." He punched Jared lightly on the arm and then headed off. Jared didn't remember to say anything until Tripp was out of earshot, but he still muttered a goodbye.

Leaning back against the wall, Jared debated what to do. He could head to the office and get his hands on Rachael's file. Ms. Post wouldn't mind him looking at a new student's information since Rachael would likely be in Jared's class. He could go find the woman and have a conversation with her, see if she said anything else surprising, though she wasn't likely going to be able to alleviate the odd feeling Jared was having. Or, he could head to the library and see if he could find anything there that might help him feel more at ease, but that didn't seem promising either. Instead of doing any of those things, Jared continued to stand in the hallway, trying to put his finger on what it was about Rachael that made him feel unsettled.

Rather than launching an investigation based on an odd feeling, he decided to let it go for the moment. When Graham came back, hopefully, he'd have a chance to speak to him. Maybe he could shed some light on the situation. If not, perhaps getting to know Rachael through class would set him at ease. Still feeling as if something strange were happening around him, Jared headed down the hallway to his office to get some work done, what he'd planned to do during his break between classes. Hopefully, whatever it was about Rachael Barnes that was leaving him unsettled would come to light soon, or else this new student might just become an obsession for him, and he didn't have time to fight vampires and unravel mysterious new vampire hunters, even if she had left every hair on the back of his neck standing on edge.

2 8

NOTHING IN THERE

Rachael

LUCK WASN'T on Rachael's side as she went back into the database to look for anything that might help her figure out what could either lock Sasha in a similar place as the one she'd recently broken out of or a weakness that could take her down once and for all. Like all vampires, a silver-tipped stake to the heart should do her in, but Sasha was strong, powerful, and fast. She was also always surrounded by an army of goons who protected her at all costs. So far, no one had been able to get the stake in, though Chell had been close once, getting her in the shoulder just before her bloodsucking hooligans were able to force the hunters away. That had been the beginning of the ongoing rivalry between Chell and Sasha. After that encounter, Chell had considered Sasha her archenemy, and the vampire had done the same. They'd tangled time and again until Chell figured out how to get rid of the vampire once and for all.

Except, now that Chell was gone, Sasha was back, and Rachael needed to find out how to stop the vampire's killing spree.

Hours passed as she looked through report after report, some of

135

them so old they'd been scanned from microfiche into the data system. Sasha had been around for ages. Rachael wondered how many lives she'd claimed in that time. So lost was she in reading all of the accounts of Sasha's murderous rampages, she ignored her growling stomach and her phone until a knock on her door alerted her that not only had she worked through lunch, it was dinner time.

Setting her laptop aside, she hurried to the door, hoping it was Graham, but she wasn't surprised when she pulled it open to see Jazz standing there, her arms folded, and a serious look on her face. "You lose your phone, girl?"

"Sorry. No. Just… busy."

"Well, Rex and me are headed down for supper. You wanna come, or are you too busy?"

Before she could answer, Rachael's stomach rumbled. Jazz grinned at her. "I'll get my phone."

"Oh, sure, now you gotta phone."

Leaving the door open so Jazz could step inside, Rachael headed back to her bedroom to grab her phone and slide her feet into her shoes. Seeing a prospective petter, Scrappy bounded across the room to Jazz's leg.

"I didn't know you had a cat," the girl said, leaning over to scratch the kitty's ears. "I didn't think we were allowed to have animals except for fish."

"They made an exception for me," Rachael explained, closing her laptop and sliding her phone into her back pocket. "Scrappy has a thing for Graham."

"Don't we all," Jazz muttered, making Rachael laugh. "I'll see you later, kitty, kitty," she said, giving the cat one last pat.

Rachael let Scrappy run her head along her leg and then breezed past her to the door, letting Jazz out first and following behind. A few seconds later, Jazz knocked on Rex's door, and without a word, he fell into step behind them. Rachael smiled at him, but he had his phone in his hands, and it was obvious he was engrossed in something else.

Once they reached the cafeteria, Rex managed to unglue the screen from his hand to get food. Rachael went through the line ahead of him, deciding it was a good night for pizza, and asked him what he'd been watching.

"More vampire videos," he confessed, taking twice as many slices of pepperoni as she had put on her plate. "Trying to see if she has a weakness."

Nodding, Rachael considered telling him she'd spent her day doing exactly the same thing but decided against it. She didn't want anyone to know she'd been using Chell's login information to access a database she wasn't supposed to know about.

They found an empty table, despite the fact that there were a lot more students in the cafeteria than there had been before. Jazz got hung up talking to a different attractive boy, and Rachael found the guy she'd been flirting with the day before, watching him carefully. He didn't look happy that Jazz was talking to this other guy, and the girl sitting next to him looked even more upset seeing him notice Jazz.

"Drama," Rachael mumbled, chuckling, but Rex had his phone out again and wasn't listening.

Eventually, Jazz made her way over, smiling about her newest conquest. She said this guy was a Lower Fall she'd met in the work-out room that morning--which was really more like noon from what Rachael could tell from Jazz's schedule. He had friends in the class that would be graduating Saturday night and asked Jazz to sit with him during the ceremony.

"I didn't even think about graduation," Rachael muttered, shaking her head. She should've been thinking about it. She was the one who had set that date….

Jazz went on, talking about the various guys she'd met, and Rachael did her best to listen, even though her mind kept wandering to the situation with Sasha--and also to Graham. It wasn't until Jazz got up to get a refill of soda that Rex lowered his phone slightly and said, "Damn, that girl talks a lot."

"Did you get a chance to talk to Tripp?" she asked, glad Rex had put his phone down long enough to speak.

He shook his head. "No, I couldn't find him before he left. I wanted to talk to him in person."

Her forehead furrowed. "I saw him in the library after lunch. He brought me my badge and a few other things."

Rex shrugged, as if it was no longer a huge concern to him that Sasha was on the loose and the trainers needed to know.

Rachael wanted to say more, but he raised his phone before she could say anything else. Deciding he must have his reasons for keeping the information to himself for now, she took a bite of her pizza, almost full, and thought about excusing herself. So far, the reports weren't doing her any good, but she was at a loss for what else might help.

Jazz was across the cafe, chatting with yet another dude. With no one to talk to and finished with her food, Rachael tossed her napkin on her tray and set her glass in the corner, ready to head back to her room.

A tap on her shoulder kept her from pushing up from the table. She turned to see familiar eyes boring into hers and held her breath. Something was up, and by the expression on Dr. McCall's face, it wasn't good.

29

HE'S SUSPICIOUS

Rachael

"Hi Rachael. How are you?" Dr. McCall asked, his hand still resting on her shoulder. "Mind if I sit?"

Rachael's eyes were wide as she attempted to formulate a response. She realized she'd shook her head when Jared pulled out the chair next to her and sat down, only a few inches away from her, as if what he wanted to say was intimate. Her eyes went to Rex. His phone was lower now, and it was clear he was observing over top of it.

"Hi… Dr. McCall," Rachael finally managed to stammer. "Is everything okay?"

"Yeah, yeah, everything is fine. I just wanted to chat with you for a minute, if you don't mind. I'm meeting a few of the other professors here for dinner in a few, but it looks like I'm early." He checked his watch, and Rachael had to wonder if his early arrival was on purpose. Not that he would've known she was there--would he?

"Rex, this is Dr. Jared McCall. He works in the history department."

"I know," Rex said, as if she was an idiot for thinking he wouldn't recognize the professor. "Hi."

"Hello, Rex," Jared said, seeming confused about whether he should offer his hand across the table. He didn't. "Are you in Lower Summer as well?"

"Yeah. I live across the hall from Rachael. You know my dad. Richard Framer."

"Oh, right!" Dr. McCall nodded his head. "We had some classes together. How's he doing?"

"Good. Keeping Nebraska safe. For the most part."

Chuckling, Dr. McCall politely said, "That's great. Richard's a good guy. I'm sure you'll be just as skilled as he is in no time."

"I think so." Rex raised his phone, signaling the conversation was over. Rachael's eyes widened as she debated whether or not to say anything to the kid. His behavior was so odd sometimes....

Her deliberations were interrupted when Jared touched her arm. "You're Wessley Barnes's granddaughter?"

"I am." Her eyebrows arched as she tried to determine where this conversation was going. "Did you know him?"

"No, I didn't. He was done at Silverwood before I started. I think he knew my grandfather, though. As a matter of fact, I think they may have done some research together. Did your grandpa ever mention him to you? Wadsworth McCall? His friends called him Worth."

The name sounded familiar for reasons Rachael couldn't understand. "Wadsworth McCall?" she repeated as Jared nodded his head, his green eyes boring into her as if he were trying to read the results of a lie detector test. "I feel like I've heard his name before, but I can't remember ever talking to Grandpa about him. To be honest, Grandpa and I weren't very close. After my parents separated, I didn't see him for a long time." She remembered the lie she'd told Graham the other day about reconnecting with Grandpa Wessley and tried to keep that in mind without making up too much now, but she truly hadn't seen the man at all since she was in elementary school. He hadn't said anything at all about the academy to her, and as far as Rachael knew, he probably died without knowing it existed--because it hadn't existed back then, had it? So why did that name, Wadsworth McCall, sound familiar?

Green eyes stared at the table for a moment as the professor contemplated a response. "All right. I was just curious. My grandfather was a bit odd. He didn't like too many people and spent most of his time holed up in his study, doing research and experiments. Your grandfather was one of the only people he confided in, and it's my understanding that Wessley helped him with some of the experiments he used to write his most famous volume. But I don't know the nature of those experiments as they aren't outlined in any of Grandfather's notes that we still have, and while his books refer to them, they aren't specific."

"Gosh, I wish I could be of more use, Dr. McCall, but Grandpa didn't say anything to me about any of that. I suppose I could call my grandma and ask her to check through the notes Grandpa left behind. Maybe we missed something...." She hoped he would say no since she hadn't spoken to her grandmother for years, certainly not about Silverwood, nor had she actually looked at any of her grandpa's notes. Wouldn't it seem strange to Grandma Esther that her granddaughter was calling her out of the blue to talk about a life Rachael wasn't supposed to be aware of?

"That's okay," Jared said, offering her a small smile. "I was just hopeful you might be able to provide a few clues as to how Grandfather Wadsworth came to his conclusions regarding his breakthrough thesis. But don't go to any trouble."

A noise at the door drew his eyes, and Rachael turned, too, to see a few of the other instructors walking in. Most of them appeared to be in their early to mid-forties, a few a little older than that. Jared was certainly the youngest, and she remembered having made him a genius who graduated early. One of the women, thin, with gray in her dark hair, waved at him, and Rachael thought that must be Dr. Carrie Ferrier, one of the other history professors.

Lifting his hand in response, Jared said, "Thanks anyway, Rachael." Then, looking into her eyes in a way that made her uncomfortable for reasons she couldn't put her finger on, he added, "I'm so glad you're here. I know you're going to be a valuable member of our team."

"Th-thanks," Rachael stammered, not sure what to make of it. Jared smiled again, an uneasy grin that seemed forced, and then got up to join the other instructors at a table reserved for staff members.

Rachael followed him across the room with her eyes, her stomach in knots. He didn't seem hostile at all, and that was what scared her. It was like he was doing his best to be her friend so that he could swoop in later and brush her legs out from under her.

"That was weird." Rex didn't lower his phone to make the comment.

Across the way, Rachael saw Jazz batting her eyes at her, even though that cute boy was still chatting her up. Rachael shook her head. Jazz had it all wrong. Dr. McCall definitely wasn't flirting. To Rex, Rachael said, "It was weird. I wish I could help him."

"Yeah, I've read that book, and it seems like the crazy scribbles of a genius gone mad to me." Rex glanced at her but then re-glued his eyes to the screen.

She let that sink in, wondering what he was talking about. Since she was only vaguely familiar with Dr. McCall's family, having only mentioned them a time or two in her novel, she was forced to ask, "What is the book even about, Rex?"

Finally setting his phone down, he shrugged. "It's a bunch of weird theories, mostly having to do with time continuums and other ideas that all sound like a bunch of rambling some old dude wrote after years of LSD use, though I don't think he was a user. I think he was just nuts. I don't know that anyone thinks any of it is real, though it would be cool if it was. It's no wonder Dr. McCall would want to see where the theories came from, though I'm sure your grandpa prob-ably thought ol' Worth was delusional, too."

"Time continuums?" The hairs on the back of Rachael's neck stood up as soon as Rex had said those words, and she didn't hear much else. "What… what's the name of the book?"

Rex answered, but he didn't have to because a memory from earlier in the day flashed before her eyes as Rachael contemplated her own question. That book, in the library, the one she'd been pretending to read. That book had been written by Dr. Wadsworth J. McCall. "Collisions of Worlds," she said at the same time as Rex.

"So you have heard of it?" Now he was confused, and she didn't blame him. So was she.

"No, but I saw it in the library today." Rachael picked up her tray, suddenly realizing she needed to go get that book. Why hadn't she thought of it before? That book--the one Jared's grandfather had written, and her own grandpa had allegedly helped with--just might contain the key to figuring out how all of this had happened.

Tray in hand, she marched across the cafeteria as Rex asked her where she was going. She didn't answer him. Ignoring Jazz's shouts of her name as she passed by, she dumped her tray and headed for the door, only vaguely aware that a pair of green eyes was following her every move.

3 0

FIND THE BOOK

Rachael

RACHAEL WASN'T sure how one was supposed to go about checking out a book when there was no librarian. There was a card in the front of the book where she could write her name and file that somewhere, like in the olden days, but she didn't want to do that either. She really didn't want anyone to know that she had the book at all. Looking for it online had been futile, and since this hardbound book was her only opportunity to actually attempt to figure out what Wadsworth McCall might know about portals and world's morphing into one another, she decided to just sit in the library and read it for a while.

She left the overhead lights off so that no one passing by would wander in to see what was going on. She even considered putting a larger book over the back cover, in case someone did come in but decided against it. The fact that Jared had said her grandfather was involved in some of the experiments or research in the book should've been reason enough for her to want to read it. Surely, she could come up with a story to explain herself should anyone question her. She was a writer after all.

A few chapters into the book, Rachael got an understanding of what Rex meant when he was discussing the book earlier. A lot of it did seem like the random ramblings of a man who'd lost his marbles. Perhaps someone with a background in physics or astronomy would've had a better chance at following what Dr. McCall the senior was attempting to say, but Rachael had neither of those things, and by the end of chapter three, she was ready to toss the book across the room. At least there seemed to be very little chance of some random reader picking up the book and discovering she'd done something to make the world in her novel collide with the world she had known up until a few days ago.

But that didn't mean Jared couldn't put the pieces together. It seemed like he was already suspicious of her for some reason. He had been nice enough when he'd come to talk to her, but there was something more there, something he wasn't saying. She could see it in his eyes.

Flipping back to the table of contents, she read through it again, trying to decide if there was a particular chapter that might offer further enlightenment as to what had happened. Perhaps something about fictional worlds coming to life, or writing oneself into a story. She saw nothing dealing with books at all. Out of frustration, she slammed the book closed and set it on the coffee table in front of her, wishing she could've kept Wadsworth McCall alive long enough to talk to him in person. Of course, had she done that, there was a good chance everyone would know what she'd done, and while she wasn't sure it mattered so much if they knew she had written the novel that became their world, she didn't want anyone to know that she was responsible for Chell's death--especially not Graham.

Thinking of him, she pulled her phone out of her pocket to make sure she hadn't missed any calls or texts. She did have one from Jazz from about twenty minutes ago, asking where she was going. She answered it quickly enough now that she saw it. "Headed to the library." That's all she needed to know for now. Jazz was probably so busy with the boys she wouldn't come looking for her. But Graham hadn't sent her a text or called.

Why would he? Just because he had stopped by her dorm room the night before, that didn't mean he was interested in her. She was just another recruit to him, one who happened to be staying in his ex-girlfriend's dorm room. That was probably his true reason for coming by, just to see if she'd destroyed the place yet. He would just love it when he saw the bedspread she'd bought--not that there was any reason why he would ever see that.

Part of her wanted to forget all of this and just head back to Baltimore, find a way to get her apartment back and all of her stuff out of storage. If she could quit Merek and Merek to become a writer in her old reality, she could do that again now, couldn't she? Granted, the story that had brought her financial independence was no longer an option. She would have to come up with another idea, something different, and she wasn't sure she had another winner. Sure, she had a million ideas for stories, but none of them were as fleshed out as this one, and she didn't have the passion to write anything else the way she did this.

Feeling defeated, Rachael took the book and walked it back over to the shelf. She could see exactly where it belonged; the hole she'd created when she pulled it out was still there. But she decided not to put it back where she'd gotten it. Instead, she moved it to another section of the library entirely, one she figured no one really used much, not that anyone used the library at all from what she could tell. Wedged between some books about calculations for measuring ingredients for spells, she figured the book would be exactly where she'd left it the next time she went looking for it, if she should ever decide to give it another try. Rachael left the library, no longer optimistic about her situation and feeling like a failure in every part of her life.

Her eyes were downcast all the way home. She might've ran into someone if there'd been anyone out and about. Once she walked into the other building, she had a good indication as to why no one was mulling around. A movie was playing in the student lounge, and from the sound of things, several people were enjoying it. She heard lots of laughter and voices seeping from around the closed doors. She wondered if Jazz was in there. It wouldn't surprise her if she was, though she doubted Rex was. He likely went back to his room to continue to study footage. Where he'd gotten any of it, she wasn't sure, but it wasn't standard YouTube postings he was watching.

There was no question Rachael wouldn't be joining the other kids. She moped her way up the stairs, eyes on her shoes, debating whether or not she should call it quits. Looking up only long enough to press her code into the door that led to their wing, she found her way to her apartment and would've ran smack into the man standing outside of her room if she hadn't seen the tips of his boots before she did so.

"You okay?" Graham asked, one hand on his hip as he looked at her, the other stroking his chin. "You look like you just lost your best friend."

Rachael thought that sounded odd coming from him, since he had recently done just that, but she didn't go there. Seeing him helped her find a smile. "I'm okay. What are you doing here?"

He shrugged as if he didn't have an answer for that. "I just got back. Grabbed some dinner. Jared mentioned he'd spoken to you about a few things, so I thought I'd stop by. But then, you weren't here, so I was going to text you. Is everything all right?"

"No," she admitted, not sure where she was going with this. Unburdening her soul and telling him everything was an option, but then, he would never be looking for her again if she did that. "I guess I'm just missing home."

"I can understand that." He gave her a sympathetic smile. "It won't be long until you feel at home here, though."

She had a feeling that might not ever be the case for her, but it was nice of him to say. Meowing on the other side of the door alerted her to the fact that her kitty was aware she was keeping her from her main squeeze. "You wanna come in for a minute? Say hello to Scrappy?" Rachael didn't think about the fact that this was his dead fiancée's room or what he might think of her for inviting him in until after the question was out of her mouth.

"Sure," Graham said, his smile changing into something else, something less sympathetic and more... friendly.

No longer concerned with the thoughts that had weighed her down on her slow march from the library, Rachael opened the door and ushered him inside.

31

HE'S IN HER ROOM

Rachael

GRAHAM LOOKED a bit uncomfortable when he initially walked into Rachael's room, but he hid it well, and when she offered him a seat on the couch and a beer, he accepted both. Scrappy pounced on his lap pretty quickly, and Rachael fought off her jealousy, wishing she was the one sitting there, having her back scratched.

"How was your trip?" she asked, taking a seat at the far end of the couch, sipping her own Bud. Wine would've been better, but without a kitchen, and a sink to wash dishes in, this would have to do. "Did you convince the recruit?"

"We didn't get as many this time around as we had hoped for. I think this will be the smallest class we've ever had. There are only seven people moving in this weekend. We weren't able to get a few that we thought we'd convinced. But it's all right. A tighter knit group will be a good thing."

He didn't sound completely convinced that what he was saying was accurate. The worry in his eyes was evident. "Are you concerned about some of the recent attacks? I'm hearing rumors they might be vampire related."

An eyebrow arched over one lavender eye. "Which ones?"

"Baltimore, especially. That family." She shrugged, trying to seem nonchalant. "Some people around here have better connections than I do and seem to think that might be significant."

Again, she could see him trying to play off his concerns. "We haven't investigated anything nearby. It might be something we need to look into."

Rachael didn't mention the marking she'd seen by the window in the video Rex had shown her, the one that indicated the slaughter was the work of Sasha Thornsby. If Graham looked into it at all, he'd make the discovery pretty quickly for himself.

Scrappy fell asleep on his lap within a few moments of him petting her, and Rachael had to laugh. He looked so uncomfortable with sleeping beauty curled up there. "It looks like Scrappy hasn't slept all day, just hoping you'd come by."

"Somehow I doubt that's the case." Graham smirked at the cat and then looked back at Rachael, still running his hands through the kitty's fur. "How was your day? You were at the library a lot, huh?"

"I was. I went earlier just to have a look around. But then, Dr. McCall mentioned my grandfather might've been working with his on a certain book, and I wanted to see if I could find it."

He nodded in understanding. "Right. He said something about that at dinner." A shadow passed over Graham's face, and Rachael assumed Jared had said some things he was questioning whether or not to share. "You weren't all that close with him, were you? Wessley?"

"No, not at all. I thought it might help for me to read something he was involved in, but…." She hesitated. The last thing she wanted was for Graham to go looking for the book and not be able to find it, as if she'd purposely hid it. "I'm not that schooled on astrophysics."

"I've read the book in question, and honestly, it didn't make a lot of sense to me. As far as I can tell, even the professors with backgrounds in similar fields have no idea what he's talking about in ninety percent of that book."

Rachael managed a small smile, but she wasn't sure whether she should admit she found the book and read part of it or not. Instead, she asked a question she thought she shouldn't ask. "Do you think it's possible? That two worlds could collide and make a new reality for everyone involved?" She took another sip of her beer, again wishing it was wine, or even something stronger, and set it on the coffee table in front of her, wishing she'd thought to bring coasters.

"I think so." Graham readjusted, causing Scrappy to stretch and roll over. He pulled his eyes off Rachael long enough to shake his head at the furry creature and then was looking at her again. "My great-grandfather said he thought that's how vampires came to be in this world in the first place, that they weren't originally part of our reality, but when they came through, it pulled their history in with ours, mingling the two."

Fascinated, Rachael leaned forward slightly on the couch so she was peering at him. "Did he have any evidence of that happening?"

"No, nothing more than the ramblings of a villager in Wallachia who swore he'd brought Vlad the Impaler to our world through a portal, that he hadn't meant to, but his made-up story of death and destruction changed into his reality one day."

Graham looked nonchalant, but Rachael could feel the hair on the back of her neck stand on end. "Do you... think that really happened?"

"I have no idea." He smirked and shrugged his shoulders. "It doesn't really matter, in my opinion. Vampires are real, they're here, and it's our job to kill them."

"But... what if it happened again? What if worlds collided another time? Or a hundred times?"

"As far as I can tell, the only one who remembered a world from before was this one guy who said he was responsible for it. That was... four hundred years ago. So... if there are more people running around out there thinking they caused worlds to collide, they aren't talking."

He had given Rachael an awful lot to think about, and he must've seen the consternation on her face. He reached his long arm over and set his hand on her bent knee where it rested between them on the couch, her foot tucked beneath her. "Rach? Are you okay?"

The feel of his palm radiated through her jeans, and once again thoughts of pushing Scrappy aside and claiming his lap for herself came to mind. The inappropriateness of such a move was obvious. Even if his fiancée hadn't recently died, she'd only known him a few days, and she was going to be here a long time if she continued in the program. It would be hard to walk away, as she'd contemplated earlier, with Graham and his heavenly cologne visiting her dorm room, even occasionally, and even for nothing more than a chat and a beer.

"I'm okay," Rachael assured him. She looked at him and found a smile. In his eyes, she could see he wasn't buying everything she was selling, but she knew him well enough to know he wouldn't ask her any more questions on the topic.

He kept his hand on her knee far longer than she expected and even rubbed her leg for a moment before he said, "I should probably go. I have a ton of appointments tomorrow. Gotta process these new recruits and get them settled in."

"Right." He pulled his hand away, and her leg suddenly felt ice cold. "Is there anything I can do to help?"

Tipping his head to the ceiling for a second, he considered an answer and then shook his head. "No, just pop out and say hi if you're around when I bring any of them by. Tripp will be doing the same. Make them feel at home. Other than Tony, they're all kids."

She remembered him mentioning the older guy. "I'm looking forward to meeting him."

Something about the narrowing of one corner of one eye made her feel like he didn't like that answer for reasons she didn't dare ponder. "I'd hate to wake your cat...."

The urge to scoop Scrappy up in her arms was overwhelming, running the backs of her arms over his muscular legs in an innocent gesture, but she didn't do it. "Scrap, come on girly, let the man go," she said, petting the top of her kitty's head.

Scrappy protested but then hopped down, discombobulated in her sleepy state. She meowed and then went straight to her bed as Graham stood and brushed a few stray hairs off his lap.

"Sorry." Rachael offered him one of the rollers she always had on hand for such incidents.

"It's okay." He didn't take it. As far as she could tell, there weren't any more stray hairs, and she was really looking. Really, really looking.

He picked up his bottle and tossed it in the trash can before heading toward the door. Rachael followed, wondering what she should say, if she should try to hug him. An air of awkwardness settled over both of them, as Graham placed a hand on the doorknob but turned back to survey the room. "This used to be Chell's room. You know that, right?"

"I do." She didn't bother to go over all the ways that she knew that information. "Does it bother you?"

"No. It did at first, but then…." He shook his head, and she could see in his eyes that he meant it. "I don't know, Rachael. I miss her like crazy, but, in some ways, I feel like she's not exactly gone. It's bizarre, and I probably sound insane even saying that out loud. But… for some reason… when I met you… I felt like I had part of her back."

Rachael met his eyes, and she could see the longing there, not for her but for understanding, and perhaps for the woman he was talking about. "It doesn't sound crazy. From what I can tell, Chell and I had a lot in common. At least, when it comes to personality. I'm not sure I will ever be able to kick vampire ass the way that she could…. But if knowing me makes you miss her a little less, then, I'm really glad I came here."

"I'm really glad you came here, too." He had turned to face her, and somehow the distance between them had narrowed during the discussion such that he was only a few inches from her now, and Rachael couldn't keep her eyes off those soft, luscious lips, the ones she'd purposely written to feel like warm embers and taste like honey.

She pressed a hand to his chest, the feel of his leather jacket heightening her sense of smell so that the manly scent he exuded had her head spinning, and he moved toward her again, letting go of the door completely, his arms moving around her, pulling her closer.

But he didn't kiss her. Instead, Graham crushed her against his chest, one hand on her back, the other wrapped around her hip. She breathed him in, felt the brush of an exhale dancing against her ear, teasing the hairs on her neck into submission. He held her for a few seconds, and Rachael let both of the worlds she'd known slip away, lost in his embrace.

When Graham stepped back, he grazed her cheek with his fingertips. "Bye, Rach."

"See you soon," she said, not sure what else might come out of her mouth, and then he was gone, out her door, leaving only a whiff of his intoxicating aroma behind for her to relish in before that, too, dissipated.

Rachael pressed her forehead to the door jamb as Scrappy, suddenly fully awake, began to rub against her leg. "What am I going to do about that man?" she whispered. The cat had no answers, and neither did she, but if Graham continued to touch her the way that he had tonight, it wouldn't be long until she'd find herself confessing her feelings to him--and possibly more, even though she knew it would be a mistake to tell him the truth. It was just about impossible to keep deceiving him, though. And if she ever wanted to find herself lying with him, she'd have to figure out a way to stop lying to him.

32

RACHAEL'S BED MAKES AN IMPRESSION

Rachael

RACHAEL AWOKE to the sound of heavy footsteps in the hallway--and chatter. The voices seemed young and energetic, which made her feel like a bum for sleeping past 9:00, but she'd stared at the ceiling for hours the night before, thinking about Graham and also about Dr. McCall the Elder's theory on world collision. So when what she assumed was the first group of fresh recruits came through, she wasn't ready to pop out into the hall to say hello. Luckily, she heard Tripp's voice pointing out the available empty rooms, so she wasn't missing out on seeing Graham.

Their presence got her booty in gear, though. She rushed through a shower and making sure Scrappy's bowls were topped off before she emptied the kitty litter and made herself presentable. Hopefully, if Graham brought a group through in the next few minutes, she'd be able to step out into the hallway under the guise of telling them all hello and see him, too.

All night, she'd wondered about the significance of that hug, the feel of his fingers on her skin as he brushed her cheek. What might've

157

happened if she'd leaned in for a kiss? Would he have done it? He had told her she reminded him of Chell, after all, which was probably because she'd written Chell a lot like herself. The character's name was even half of her own.

But she wasn't Chell, especially not to the other people who had actually known her--like Graham. And Sammi. She couldn't expect to step into this world and suddenly be someone else. She couldn't expect Graham to just forget he'd been engaged to what he thought was the love of his life only to have her taken away. And if he ever found out that Rachael was responsible for her demise, she wouldn't be able to expect him to just forgive her, either. She'd written him to be an understanding, sympathetic person, but not crazy, and that's probably what it would take to just forgive someone who was responsible for your fiancée's death.

She decided to eat a breakfast bar rather than trek down to the cafeteria, just in case she missed Graham coming by. She realized she hadn't even turned the television on since she arrived, but since she wanted to be able to hear activity in the hallway, she sat on the couch and stared at the wall while she ate, eventually taking her phone out of her pocket so that she could read. It had been a long time since she'd checked out any of the other books on WebReader, so she went there to see what the new number one was. A book about werewolves. "Nice," she muttered. "Maybe I should message the author and let him know it's a bad idea to kill off the main character and then put yourself in the book." The idea of a bunch of werewolves running around on top of the vampires made her stomach unsettled.

Rachael didn't actually send the email, though she did read for a few minutes before she heard more voices in the hallway. It was obvious to her now why Jazz slept with a fan on, and she thought she might have to try that if there were going to be so many people coming and going at all hours. Locking that thought away for later, she hopped up off the couch and strode to the door.

His voice echoed down the hall before she saw him, and Rachael found herself leaning against the door jamb with a wide smile on her face before Graham's tall form even came into view. He was walking backward, talking to a group of four or five kids--Rachael didn't pull her eyes away from him to check. Instead, she let her imagination carry her away again, imagined her fingers running through his thick, dark hair, her face pressed to his neck, those arms around her again....

Lavender eyes flickered before hers, and she realized he had turned around and was talking to her now. "Good morning, Rach." One eyebrow was cocked just enough to make her wonder if she'd been daydreaming too loudly. Had he read her thoughts? "How are you this morning?"

"Good, good." She focused on the others for the first time. There were four of them. Two young girls, a boy who made Rex look like a grown man, and a guy who could've been Rachael's older brother by the looks of him. That had to be Tony. He was definitely older than the others, probably Graham's age, but not what she'd envisioned when she'd heard his name. Muscular didn't quite do the man justice--his muscles had muscles. His bald head gleamed in the hall light, and though he wasn't tall, he was definitely powerful. His eyes were a clear shade of blue, almost like ice with a streak of sky. It suddenly dawned on her why Graham had been slightly defensive the night before at the mention of the new student. He was hot--and he was looking at her with a Joey Tribbiani smile.

"I'd like for all of you to meet Rachael Barnes. She just moved in a few days ago and will be in your class."

"Our class?" one of the girls echoed. She was blonde and looked more than a little lost, but one side of her face pulled up in a snarl as she looked Rachael up and down.

"Yes. I'm a nontraditional student," Rachael explained.

"Does that mean old?" the blonde asked.

Rachael's eyebrows raised, but she didn't have to reply. "Hey, there, kid watch yourself," Tony joked, nudging the girl lightly in the shoulder before he approached Rachael with his hand out. "Hey there, Rach. I'm Tony, Tony Espisito. Man, is it nice to meet you." He looked her up and down in a way that made Rachael feel like a piece of meat hanging in a butcher shop--only somehow in a good way, which she couldn't quite sort out. She took his hand and heard a low grumble from Graham.

"It's nice to meet you, too, Tony." She didn't look at Graham or acknowledge the sound he'd just made, and if Tony heard it, he didn't either. "I take it you're also a little older than the high school graduates."

"Yeah, yeah. But I ain't thirty yet." He chuckled and finally let go of her hand. "Glad to have a babe on the floor who's not fresh out of glee club."

Rachael felt her face go warm, but before she could reply, Graham stepped in. "Rachael, this is Belinda Shields." The blonde--she waved but didn't step over. Rachael forced a smile and waved back, mentally checking the "do not like" box in her mind. "This is Karma Malone."

"Hi," Karma, a petite Latina with curves waved, and Rachael instantly liked her. She had a friendly smile and dark hair the color of a raven's feathers. It fell down her back, almost reaching her waist.

"It's nice to meet you," Rachael said, meaning it for once.

"And this is Doug Cooper."

Doug did not seem to belong. Wiry with glasses and hair so chopped up in front, it looked as if his mother must've cut it, she had a feeling he'd get eaten alive by his classmates or trainers before the vampires even had a chance.

By the expression on his face, Doug looked like he knew that, too. He lifted a hand in a self-conscious wave, and Rachael said, "Hi, Doug. Nice to have you here." She swallowed hard and then returned her attention to Graham who seemed to be trying to figure out how to get Tony to take more than a step away from her. Rachael wasn't used to seeing anyone be jealous of someone giving her attention, but she liked it on Graham, even though he didn't wear it well.

"Can we see your room?" Karma asked. "My parents are bringing my stuff later this afternoon. It'd be great to have an idea of the layout."

"Sure," Rachael replied, pushing the door open all the way. Scrappy took her opportunity to dart to Graham's leg, and she heard him utter a curse word as the new recruits came in.

She let them mill about freely, having nothing to hide, assuming Tony didn't open her underwear drawer. Rachael scooped up her cat. With the others in her apartment, she was alone in the hall with Graham for a second. "Sorry about Scrappy," she said, standing only inches from him and looking into his eyes.

He shook his head, one side of his mouth pulling up into a grin. "It's okay. I just don't get why she likes me so much."

"What's not to like?"

Graham's smile widened, but before he could respond, she heard Karma exclaim, "Oh, cool. You get your own bathroom."

Rachael grinned at him and then walked inside, fielding questions from the newbies for a few minutes as she tried to keep track of where all of them had gone. Tony was dangerously close to her drawers, and she imagined him looking inside if she turned her back on him for a few seconds. She held Scrappy in her arms to keep her off Graham, and Belinda whined that she didn't get to bring her cat, Fluffy.

Graham stayed in the living room area for the first few minutes but eventually followed Doug in beyond the divider. Rachael had her back to him and was talking to Karma about the water pressure when she heard him gasp.

Turning around, she realized he was fixated on her bed. His eyes were wide, and all of the color seemed to be draining from his face. Without a word, he backed into the living room. Rachael was certain no one else had noticed, but she felt like an idiot for letting him wander in there and see that bedspread with all of the new recruits around. For that matter, she felt stupid for having bought it in the first place. She should've known better.

But he didn't know she had any idea what would've made him react that way, and she had to keep that in mind for the next time she spoke to him.

It didn't take long for him to decide they needed to move on. It was clear when she walked back into the living room he wanted out of the dorm at all costs. Rachael feigned confusion, and he smiled at her reassuringly, as if to say that everything was fine, but she knew better--she would've known better even if she wasn't aware of what had caused him to react that way. In a matter of minutes, he had the newbies moving on down the hall and didn't stop to point out anything else in Lower Summer.

Rachael went back into her apartment and let Scrappy go, feeling like a jerk. She ran her hands down her face and tried to get a grip on herself. After what had happened last night, and Graham admitting she reminded him of Chell, the last thing she needed was for it to seem creepy--and having bought the exact same bedspread as his ex was probably not a good way to keep things innocent.

She walked over to the sofa and sank into the cushions, wondering what her next move should be. Would he ever even want to come back to her apartment knowing what was on the other side of the screen? She hoped so, but she couldn't blame him if Graham never walked through the door again.

3 3

LOOKING FOR MORE

Rachael

RACHAEL SPENT most of the day digging around online, looking for more information about Sasha, reading reports, and looking at footage of Chell and Sasha fighting taken from other teammates. It was insane to watch some of the battle scenes she'd actually scripted take shape in front of her eyes. Perhaps even crazier was thinking that the trainers were actually going to attempt to teach her how to do that as well.

She didn't see Graham again before the graduation ceremony. At dinner, she'd spent most of the time looking around for him but coming up short. Jazz was rambling on about the guy she was supposed to sit with, and Rex had his phone up in front of his eyes, so all Rachael could do was sit and nod and try not to think about Graham, which wasn't happening.

It didn't help that Jared seemed to be looking at her every single time she glanced in his direction. He'd smiled and waved earlier, but it didn't seem that sincere. He looked nice, dressed in a suit and tie, one slightly more dressy than what he normally wore to class. It made her assume that he would be going straight to the gym for graduation once he was done with dinner.

Rachael was not. She had a dress picked out for the occasion but hadn't put it on before she went to eat, afraid she'd get something on it. So, after she finished her pasta, she headed back to her dorm to get dressed. Hoping she'd have a chance to see Graham, maybe even ask him what had happened earlier--as if she didn't know--she put on an extra spritz of a floral perfume that was similar to the one Chell had worn but not exactly the same. She was done trying to be exactly like Chell.

The bleachers in the gym were pulled down, and when she walked in, there were already dozens of people seated. On the gym floor, there were about thirty chairs for the students arranged facing the podium, and seats for the staff as well, split evenly on either side of where the speaker would stand.

Glancing around, she tried to decide where to sit. She could attempt to sit with other people, get to know them, or take a spot by herself. She was just about to do the latter when she saw Karma lift her hand. Realizing the girl was looking at her, Rachael decided to join her Lower Summer classmates, even though Belinda didn't look thrilled to see her. Tony was smiling from ear to ear, and Doug looked slightly less uncomfortable than he had earlier. There were three other people with them she hadn't met yet. Before she reached them, she sent a text to Rex to let him know they were all sitting together--except for Jazz who was on some sort of an odd date. Rachael saw her further down the bleachers chatting up that guy from the cafe.

"Hi, Rachael!" Karma said, hugging her as she stepped into the row. "You look so beautiful. That shade of blue is really your color!"

Rachael glanced down at the dress she was wearing, as if she couldn't remember having picked it out a few hours ago. It was sleeveless with a fitted skirt that came to her knee, though a layer of sheer fabric in the same shade of cobalt blue covered that. She felt beautiful in it.

"Thanks, girl. You look cute, too." Karma had on a hot pink top and nice black dress pants. She thanked her, and then Rachael greeted the boys. Tony winked at her, and Doug's hand was sweaty, but they were pleasant. Belinda just waved from the other side of Tony without stretching for her hand.

"This is Nick, Georgia, and Brit." Karma introduced the three classmates she hadn't met yet. They were all nice and shook her hand. Nick had to have just graduated from high school, but he looked like he probably played sports, maybe football, and Rachael thought Jazz was going to be upset she was missing out. Georgia was a red-headed southern beauty queen, and Brit was a thin blonde with stringy hair who looked like she either didn't care too much about her appearance or hadn't had a mother-figure to teach her. Maybe she just didn't know what to do with herself.

The group chatted for a few minutes, getting acquainted. Rachael fielded several questions because she'd been there a few days longer-- and also because she had created the entire place, though they obviously didn't know that. Rex came in and silently sat down behind her, phone in hand, so she didn't introduce him yet. After a few minutes, a hush fell over the crowd as the staff came in and took their seats by the podium. Dr. Overbranch walked in last and stood behind the podium. The science and history professors were on one side while the trainers took their place on the other. Rachael strained her neck looking for other staff members--no one in particular of course--and then realized they were sitting on the front row of the bleachers. Leaning as far forward as she could, she tried to catch a glimpse of Graham, but it wasn't until they stood to welcome in the graduates that she saw him. He was facing away from her, but even from behind, and just seeing the back of his head, he looked unbelievably hot.

Wearing black robes with red cords, the thirty new grads walked in, all smiles and ready to go out into the world to show what they'd learned. Rachael tried to concentrate on the ceremony, but she spent much of the time wiggling around on the bleacher, trying to get a better view of Graham. She was in trouble--serious trouble.

The valedictorian of the class was a large dude with a long beard and some girth in his shoulders. Rachael realized she knew him before he even started talking. His name was Roger Rush, and she'd created him last year when she was writing about some of the students going on a training hunt that went badly. It was crazy listening to him speak when all of the words that had ever come out of his mouth and reached her ear before now had originally been hers.

He started off talking about the privilege of being at the academy, but then the speech grew dark as he began to talk about Chell and how honored he was to get to know and work with her. By the time he finished speaking, everyone had tears in their eyes--and Graham was headed out the door.

Rachael's first instinct was to follow him. She started to get up off the bleacher, but something was holding her there. At first, she couldn't figure out what it was until she looked up and realized it was Sammi Knight's stare. From her seat near the podium, she was glaring across the space, and the darts coming out of her eyes had Rachael paralyzed and unable to pull herself up off her seat to follow the man whose heart she'd inadvertently broken. Whether it was magic, hate, or both, Rachael wasn't sure, but she wasn't going anywhere.

RUNNING INTO HIM

Rachael

THE STUDENT LOUNGE was crowded even though the party there was meant mostly for non-traditional students and those whose families hadn't come for the ceremony. Of the thirty graduates, only three fit into that category. But many of the students still in the program were there for cake, punch, and other beverages--if they were old enough. The room was decorated in red and silver, the academy's colors, with streamers, balloons, and matching tablecloths, etc. Rachael didn't spend too much time taking it all in, though. She was looking for Graham, but his face wasn't in the crowd.

He'd come back into the gym briefly to see the students receive their diplomas, but he'd stood by the door, not moving toward the rest of the faculty, and not staying for the end of the ceremony. As soon as the last student was done, he'd bailed again. Rachael hadn't even contemplated following him at that point even without Sammi's eyes boring through her. She'd learned her lesson.

But this was different. She was leaning against the wall pretending to listen to Jazz talk about what a snooze her date had been. Belinda,

Brit, and Karma were entertained at least. It seemed like Belinda could get on board with Jazz. Maybe Rachael could like the girl after all if Jazz could turn her into an ally. The boy in question was across the room with some of the upperclassmen, and he didn't look as if he'd enjoyed his time with Jazz either. What one could gather about a person from sitting on the bleachers next to them at a graduation ceremony was beyond Rachael, but she was sure Jazz would recover and move on soon enough.

Checking the time, she saw that it was 8:30. The ceremony had ended over a half-hour ago. She'd congratulated the three hunters who were attending the party, each of which would be going back to their hometowns across the country to join local teams, and then fell into this conversation. Even if she couldn't find Graham, standing here seemed to be sucking her life away as surely as any set of fangs could do.

Rachael fake yawned, really throwing herself into it. Apparently, she'd overdone it because Jazz stopped talking to look at her. "Sorry. I'm just... tired."

"You don't say?" the girl asked, smirking. "Anyway, all he could talk about was *Star Wars*. I mean, don't get me wrong, I like *Star Wars*, but I don't want to talk about it all damn night."

"You know... I think I'm gonna head back to my room." Rachael had to wait for Jazz to take a breath to slide that in. "I'm beat."

"It's only 8:30," Karma reminded her.

"Yeah, but she's old." Belinda rolled her eyes.

Though tempted to put the girl in her place, Rachael just ignored her. "I was up late last night. You kids have fun." When she said kids, she looked right at Belinda--who rolled her eyes again.

Cutting through the crowd, she dropped the drink she'd been holding into the trash and made her way out the door, only to take two steps and freeze. "Dr. McCall. We've got to stop meeting like this." Jared was headed back into the lounge from the looks of it.

He chuckled softly and pulled on his tie as if it was strangling him. "Hi, Rachael. How are you?"

"I'm good." She had a feeling he could read her mind somehow, to see that she was lying, that she was a total fraud. Swallowing hard, she asked, "How are you?"

"Well, thank you. I see I have you in class starting Monday. I'm looking forward to it. It'll be a small group, so we should all get to know each other well."

"I'm looking forward to it, too." She wasn't--she really wasn't. Even though she'd loved Jared when he was a figment of her imagination, now that he was real and standing in front of her, he made her so nervous, she felt as if her fingernails were vibrating.

"Where are you headed? Back to the library?"

There was a threat or a dare or something in that question, despite his smile. Rachael choked on her own saliva, her throat feeling restricted. "Uh... no. I was going to go to my room, but I thought I might get some fresh air first. It was... stuffy in there."

He nodded. "Well, I hope you have a good night, Rach."

"Thanks. You, too." She started to walk around him when he spoke again, causing her feet to adhere to the tile.

"By the way, Rachael, did you find the book? The other night? When you went to the library?"

Slowly she turned to look at him. "The book?"

"Yeah, my grandfather's book. The one your grandpa helped him with. Did you find it?"

"I... uh...." How did he know she'd gone to the library to read that damn book? If she lied, would he know that, too? Would he know she'd put it on the wrong shelf? "Yeah... I found it. But it didn't make a whole lot of sense to me."

He nodded, his smile looking as if it had gone through the wash a few times, it was so faded. "Well, if you have any questions, maybe I can help. I've read it a few times. I don't have all of the answers. But the pieces are starting to come together."

Rachael's eyes bulged as she realized, once again, he was saying more than his words conveyed. "Thanks. I'll... remember that."

"Good. Yes, you should remember that." Jared didn't look at her when he spoke, and then he walked into the lounge, not acknowledging her again.

Holding her breath, Rachael stared after him for a moment and then pivoted toward the exit, letting her feet carry her to open air as quickly as possible. Clearly, Dr. Jared McCall knew more about who she was and what had happened than he was willing to tell her. Rachael had to find a way to win him over before her world came crashing down around her. Again.

35

A QUIET PLACE

Rachael

GULPING FRESH AIR, Rachael looked around the courtyard and tried to figure out what to do next. She was glad to get away from Jared McCall's penetrating gaze, but she had no idea where to go or how she was going to handle the situation. Whether he actually knew something or was just suspicious, she wasn't sure. Either way, she wanted to put some space between the two of them until she had a better plan in place so that she could show Dr. McCall she wasn't so bad... for a murderer.

Realizing she hadn't spent much time outside looking around, Rachael decided to take advantage of the relatively cool evening. A light breeze was blowing, and the sky was lit by a thousand stars she hadn't ever seen while living in the big city. The grounds were expansive, with wooded areas and gardens in the back. She headed off the main path down a row of pavers toward the scent of roses and a view of petals illuminated by the full moon beyond a brick garden wall.

The flowers smelled wonderful, and she remembered how she'd added this area not only to beautify the campus but to give Chell a place to come and sit and think about life. So she shouldn't have been too surprised when she rounded a row of hedges to see the bench Chell used to sit on was occupied.

Graham had his head in his hands and was staring at the space between his feet. His tie was on the bench next to him, his white shirt undone at least three buttons down as if the silver tie had been a noose. His breathing was steady, but she imagined he'd come here to cry, to think about Chell, to curse the one who'd cost his beloved her life.

Rachael wanted to tear herself away and give him some privacy, but with the moonlight glistening in his hair, his muscular form straining against his suit jacket, that vulnerable position she'd found him in, the temptation to reach out, to provide any sort of comfort she could, was overwhelming, and she couldn't seem to pull herself away, no matter how hard she tried.

He must've felt the heaviness in her gaze because he glanced up and saw her standing there. Rachael still didn't move. One hand on the hedge, her feet split in a frozen step, she looked into his eyes and waited for him to tell her to go away.

Graham didn't do that, though. He wiped a hand down his face and quietly asked, "How long have you been standing there?"

It wasn't what she'd expected. "Not long. A few seconds. I'm sorry. I didn't mean to disturb you. I just needed some air."

"No, it's okay." He found a smile and pressed his palm to the back of his neck. Rachael found herself able to move again and took a step back, folding her hands in front of her. "You don't have to go."

"Are you sure? It looks like you want to be alone."

His smile became more genuine, and she saw a spark in his eyes. "No, it's fine. I wouldn't mind the company. Your company, anyway."

Trying not to read more into that than was necessary, Rachael stepped over and took a seat on the side away from where he'd slung his tie. They sat in silence for several minutes, gazing up at the sky. "I can't get over how beautiful it is out here." She'd written it that way, of course. The idea had slipped her mind until that moment, that she'd written the sky over Silverwood Academy to be mesmerizingly beautiful. The thought that she could somehow control the heavens seemed absurd, and yet she was seeing it above her in all of its splendor now. A shooting star flashed by, and she had to wonder, if she'd written aliens, would those somehow exist, too?

"It's gorgeous," Graham agreed. "Chell used to come here a lot. I kind of thought it was a waste of time in a way, just sitting, looking at the sky, smelling the flowers. But... now that she's gone, when I'm here, I feel closer to her." The glistening of tears were evident in his eyes as he dropped his gaze level with the horizon.

Rachael put her hand on his arm, ignoring the tingle touching him sent down her spine. "I can't imagine how difficult this is for you, Graham. I'm so very sorry that Chell is gone."

He turned his face to look at her, a crooked grin pulling at one side of his mouth. "It's not your fault."

She swallowed hard. If he only knew the truth.... "Still, no one should have to go through that. From what I've heard, she was a remarkable person, not someone who can just be replaced." Rachael hoped to make it clear that wasn't what she was trying to do either-- even if it was exactly what she was trying to do.

Unexpectedly, Graham slid closer to her. His strong arm draped over her shoulders, and she found her head cradled in the crook of his neck. He tipped his head down so that his forehead was resting on her crown, and took a few slow, deep breaths while she tried not to breathe--tried not to relish in that scent that was so completely intoxicating, so completely Graham Halloway.

He held her for several moments. The awkwardness seeped away eventually, and Rachael relaxed into his arms, wrapping hers around his waist. It was a dangerous game she was playing, attempting to pass her longing off as comfort, but she couldn't help herself. It felt so right, being there in his arms, the skin of her cheek pressed against his neck, his face in her hair. The temptation to lift her face and find his lips was overwhelming, but she resisted, reminding herself that his feelings for her were not the same, that he hardly knew her.

Graham pulled his arm away slowly and lifted his head. Reluctantly, Rachael let him go, keeping space between them. "Thank you, Rachael."

"You're welcome, Graham." She smiled at him, fighting her fingers that wanted nothing more than to trace the strands of his hair where they peaked above those inquisitive eyes. "I should probably go."

"Yeah, okay. I'll walk you back."

"You don't have to." As much as she would've continued to enjoy his company, she didn't want to have him at her door again, have to fight the urge to press her lips to his.

"Okay. I'll see you tomorrow."

She smiled and slid off the bench, pausing to look at him over her shoulder as she followed the meandering path back toward the dorm building.

Once she was out of the garden, Rachael ran a hand through her hair and blew out a hot breath. Did Graham have any idea what effect he had on her, and if he did, would he continue to instigate these encounters--or was he completely innocent? She wasn't sure, but part of her was ready to find out. The other part just wanted to appreciate it for what it was and give the man some time. In the end, she figured she'd do something to rush it and end up ruining any possibility of Graham ever truly liking her. Patience was a virtue Rachael Barnes was unfamiliar with.

3 6

CLASS BEGINS

Rachael

RACHAEL'S first class started at 9:00, but she was up and ready to head out by 8:00, so she decided to stop by the cafeteria, even though she didn't much feel like socializing. Her stomach was in knots as she worried about sitting in Dr. McCall's class the first day. Thankfully, she made it through breakfast without having to talk much since Rex was the only one in the cafe she knew, and he never said much of anything.

"What's your first class?" Rachael asked him as they finished up their waffles.

"History with Dr. McCall."

Letting out a sigh of relief, Rachael said, "Mine, too." It would be nice to have a friend in class. Not that there were too many people in their group she didn't like, but she hadn't met all of them yet, and Belinda was sure to give her a hard time if they had any classes together. That girl could be so rude.

"You wanna walk together?" Rex asked. It was possibly the longest sentence he'd formed in days.

"Yeah, sure." Rachael took her tray up and then came back for her backpack. They had no textbooks, so she only had a notebook, a pen, a bottle of water, and her laptop. She knew the professors liked to get to know their students on the first day, so there was a good chance she wouldn't need any of that, but she liked being prepared.

"Who do you have for science?" she asked as she walked alongside Rex through the open walkway to the other building.

"Dr. Stranger. I have my PE rotation in-between, though."

Rachael shook her head at the name--she'd picked that name, of course, Blaze Stranger. It sounded so dumb now. "Are you with Flint for training?" She assumed he had to be since Flint Tork and Marcy Star were assigned to the newbies.

"Yeah. What time do you go to the gym?"

"After science." Rachael had been glad to see that she had her training session last so that she could go home and shower if she wanted to. "I have Dr. Mellow." Again--silly name. Jana Mellow. The song "They Call it Mellow Yellow" came to mind, and Rachael cursed herself, thinking she'd be singing it all damn day.

Dr. McCall was standing outside of the classroom greeting his new students as they arrived. Rachael assumed there would only be about four in her class since there were so few of them to begin with and they had three different options for courses at the time. She was excited not to have too many people in each class so she could have more individualized instructional opportunities, but she didn't like the fact that she'd have nowhere to hide when Dr. McCall's eyes fell on her.

"Rex, Rachael," he said with a smile, offering Rex his hand first. "Welcome to Vampire History 101." Rex only smiled uneasily and then stepped into the room. Dr. McCall took her hand, his smile shifting slightly, as if he were more comfortable with her--or he wanted her to think they were friends. "Good morning."

"Good morning, Dr. McCall." Rachael smiled, trying to pretend sweat wasn't pouring down the back of her legs, dripping like a football coach who'd just gotten a Gatorade celebration.

Another student came up behind her, giving Rachael a chance to walk into the class. Tony jumped out of his seat the second he saw her. "Well, if it isn't Ray Ray! How you doin' girl?" He hugged her, and the overpowering scent of his cologne almost made her cough.

"I'm good, Tony. Thanks," she managed, mentally noting no one had ever called her Ray Ray before. He was the only other student in the class, but Dr. McCall was still chatting with Georgia.

Rachael sat down next to Tony on the front row, right in front of Dr. McCall's desk, because it seemed silly to sit anywhere else when there would be so few students in the class. Rex was sitting a few seats away near the window.

"Come on in," Dr. McCall said to Georgia, ushering her inside and closing the door behind her. "This is it. I can't remember the last time I had such a small group, but I'm looking forward to getting to know each of you better."

Georgia smiled at Rachael and then took a seat on the other side of Tony. It seemed so odd that Rex was off by himself, but Dr. McCall didn't ask him to move. Instead, he sat on the corner of his desk and said, "Before we start talking about vampires, let's get to know each other a little better. I wanna know everything I can about each of you because that will help me understand exactly what it is I can do to help you. If I don't know you well, I can't do that, and more than anything else, my job is to assist each of you in becoming the best vampire hunters you can be."

"As you have already noticed, our enrollment numbers are down. That's not too unusual for a summer class, but these numbers are surprisingly low. Less vampire hunters means each of us has to work even harder. But I assure you, if you put in the time and effort over the next two years while you're at Silverwood, when you leave here, you'll be ready to face any bloodsucker head on. So… let's take some time and introduce ourselves. I have a feeling the four of you are going to be a tight knit group soon enough." He smiled and looked at each of them, and Rachael did her best to smile back, but he was still making her super uncomfortable. "Georgia, do you want to go first?"

"Sure. I'm Georgia Cline. I'm eighteen years old, and I'm from Boone, North Carolina. I was planning on going to college to get my teaching degree, but when Tripp showed up and told me all about this place, he had me changin' my mind pretty quick. I guess it's been a while since anyone in my family's done this for a livin'. But I'm really lookin' forward to it--and gettin' to know you all." Her smile was like a sunbeam on a cloudy day, and Rachael couldn't help but think she sure was cute.

"Perfect. We're happy to have you, Georgia. Tony?"

"Well, I'm Tony Espisito. I'm a little older than Georgie here." That got a chuckle, though Georgia looked a little stunned at the nickname. "I was a personal trainer in Orange County C.A. up until a few days ago. All of this seemed crazy to me till I call my old man, and he says it's true--his old man used to hunt the undead. So I figure, what the hay? What do I got to lose, you know?"

"Excellent. Thanks, Tony. Rachael?"

Dr. McCall's eyes were hyper-focused on her face, which made Rachael want to fake a stomach ache and take off. "Uh… I'm Rachael Barnes. I'm twenty-five. I used to be an accountant, but apparently my Grandpa Wessley used to be a vampire hunter. I quit my job at an accounting firm in Baltimore and decided to give this new life a try." She smiled like that was all there was to it. Jared held her gaze for a long moment.

"Thank you, Rachael." He seemed as if he was hoping she'd say more, but she wasn't volunteering anything, and she certainly wasn't going to mention writing. "And Rex?"

"Rex Framer. Seventeen. Hastings, Nebraska. Both of my parents are hunters."

Jared's eyebrows raised. "Very succinct. Thanks, Rex. As all of you know by now, I'm Dr. Jared McCall. I don't care if you call me Jared or Dr. McCall, but I only let my teammates get away with calling me Doc." That got a chuckle out of everyone except Rex who looked disinterested. "I come from a long line of vampire hunters and have been associated with the academy my whole life. I graduated from high school early and subsequently graduated from here and got my doctorate in history before I turned twenty-five, and I've been teaching history here for the last six years."

"So you're thirty-one?" Georgia asked.

"Ah, and we have a mathematician," Dr. McCall joked. "Yes, I am. I am the youngest instructor in the classroom, though there are a couple of trainers who are younger than me, and both of your recruiters as well, although Tripp only has a few months on me. Any other questions about my old age?"

Again, three students laughed, and Rex stared unblinking.

"In this class, you will learn everything we know about the history of vampires, dating back to our first historical recordings of their existence. We'll talk about origin theories, social relations in clans, and also get into weaponry and techniques that have historically been effective against them. Since there are only four of you, we'll have plenty of opportunities for discussion and sharing ideas. I think you will enjoy this class, and it shouldn't be difficult for any of you to pass, but if you ever need anything, please feel free to come and talk to me any time. Now, I will hand out the syllabus, and we'll discuss how to download your textbook."

Rachael hadn't been in a classroom for years and never imagined she'd be here again, but she was actually enjoying herself. Dr. McCall's syllabus looked easy enough. There were chapters to read each week, a schedule of assignments and tests, and only three short papers. Those would be a breeze.

The time seemed to fly by quickly, and before she knew it, class was over. "I will see you all next time," Dr. McCall said as they stood and gathered their belongings. Rachael was already thinking about her science class when she heard Jared say, "Rachael could I speak to you for just a second?"

Facing away from him, she rolled her eyes and tried not to give away her disdain. "Sure."

The others left before he said a word, but when they were alone, Dr. McCall asked quietly, "What do you like to do in your spare time, Rachael?"

She stared at him blankly, trying to think of a suitable answer. "Why do you ask?"

He shrugged. "Just trying to get to know you better."

"Well... I like to read. I go for walks. Of course, I spend a lot of time with my cat.... I talk to my mom on the phone almost every night. Not since I got here, though. I don't know. That's about it."

He nodded slowly. "You say you like to read?"

"Yes...."

"Do you also like to write?"

She held her breath for a moment. Why in the world had he asked her that? "I don't know. I guess so."

Dr. McCall continued to hold her gaze for a few seconds before a faux smile spread across his face. "All right. Thanks, Rach. See you soon."

She arched an eyebrow. Soon? What did that mean? "Yep. See you soon." Rachael hurried out the door before he had a chance to call her back. He knew something--for sure. But exactly what he had figured out, she didn't know, nor did she have any idea what he might do with that information. She had a feeling it wouldn't be good.

37

MORE CLASSES

Rachael

JAZZ WAS in the same science class as Rachael, which would've been fun if she would've stopped talking for a few moments in order to give Rachael a chance to breathe before Dr. Mellow started class. One of the students she hadn't met yet was with them, a guy named Colton. With Doug, that was their entire class. There was only one other student in Lower Summer she hadn't met yet, a girl named Krista. She had been in Jazz's training program first thing in the morning, and her friend liked her enough to talk about her for a solid five minutes. Rachael only half listened as her mind kept wandering back to Dr. McCall's question. Why had he asked her if she liked to write?

"Good morning, students," Dr. Mellow said as she stepped to the center of the front of the room. She was a thin, middle-aged woman, with graying brown hair pulled into a bun on the back of her head. She wore a long yellow, cotton skirt, a white shirt, and the same gray sweater Rachael knew she wore every day. It was her classroom sweater she only put on when she was cold, and since she was so thin and petite, she was almost always cold. "Welcome to Scientific Processing 101. I'm Dr. Jana Mellow. Unlike some of the professors, I prefer to be called Dr. Mellow." She shrugged. "I grew up in a time when we spoke to our professors with respect. Now, some of these younger instructors want to be your friend." Her smile wasn't unfriendly, but her words were clear. "I am not here to be your friend. I'm here to teach you how to use your minds to open up possibilities beyond what you've ever thought imaginable."

She went on to discuss how Graham Silverwood discovered several hundred years ago that there were powers in the mind that could be unlocked through certain methods, that these powers had been known to mankind back in the Middle Ages, but had been lost. Now, not only was magic alive and well, it was more advanced than ever before.

Rachael knew the history of how magic had come to be rediscovered. She'd explained all of that back when Chell had first started her classes. She also knew Dr. Mellow was about to discuss supplements the students would begin taking soon that would help them to find their magic. When Rachael had originally thought up these supplements, she'd been careful to explain to readers that they weren't drugs--this wasn't LSD or anything. Now, as Dr. Mellow explained it… they sounded a little bit like drugs. She checked the faces of the other students, and they were mystified. The recruiters didn't say much about magic, so this was information they had yet to wrap their minds around.

Dr. Mellow handed out the syllabus to her stunned students and asked if there were any questions. There were tons. What sort of powers might they have? How long would it take for them to develop? Would it be hard? Would it be painful? Were there side effects to these supplements? Were they legal? Why didn't anyone else know about these? Rachael asked a question or two herself so she'd fit in. No need to alert anyone that she might be a bit different than the others. Dr. Mellow answered all of them succinctly, usually with only a few words and a promise to get into it more later. It all seemed a bit like "Harry Potter" now that she was sitting in a student desk watching it all unfold.

Answering questions took the majority of their class time, but Dr. Mellow wasn't one for letting her students go early. "Now, let us delve into the realm of scientific probabilities." She turned to the blackboard and picked up a piece of chalk. With the screech of the chalk along the board, Rachael desperately wished she'd updated the classrooms. White boards and overhead projectors would've been a nice touch--and not nearly as irritating to the ear.

Dr. Mellow preferred lecture to discussion, so she began by going over the different zones of the brain and how those zones could be accessed through the methods she would teach. "First, we will discuss the parts of the brain in detail. You must know them before you can utilize them efficiently. Now, let's talk about the amygdala."

For the next few minutes, Dr. Mellow lectured about the brain, and the students took notes. Rachael's main note was to make any other professors she ever created less boring. When it was finally time to go, she was almost looking forward to it--until she realized she had training next. Chances were, Sammi would be in the gym as well, and she wasn't looking forward to that, especially since she'd already had a run in with Dr. McCall that day.

"Whatcha got next, Rach?" Jazz asked her in the hall.

"Training."

"Oh. Well, at least you won't be fallin' asleep." She rolled her eyes and looked over her shoulder at the classroom door they'd just exited.

"Was it Lower Fall in with you?"

"Yep. Sammi and Ty are so opposite. It was odd listening to them run their students through their training. He's all sweet as honey, and she's barkin' at them. Craziness. Marcy was cool, though. You'll like her. And Flint was tough but encouraging."

"Great." Rachael faked a smile. At least she'd be prepared to walk into the gym and see Sammi there.

"Don't worry, girl. You got this. You've already got one of the profs thinkin' you're cute and the primary recruiter. I'm sure you can make it through the academy with flying colors with those two on your side."

Rachael stopped walking. "What? What--did you say? What in the world makes you think...."

"Save it, girl. Don't pretend you don't know what I'm talkin' about. Everyone sees it." Jazz winked and then took a few steps backward. "I gotta go see your favorite professor. See you later." She smiled sweetly and headed toward Dr. McCall's classroom, leaving Rachael staring after her with her mouth hanging open.

Everyone knew it? Why did everyone know any of that since it wasn't true--especially the part about Dr. McCall? If anything, he wanted to call her out as a fraud and let the world know she'd murdered Chell. And Graham... well, she could sort of see why there might be rumors about them--unfounded ones. Still, the fact that "everyone" was talking about her was unsettling. Now wasn't the time to be discombobulated either, not with Sammi on the horizon. Rachael took some deep breaths and tried to calm down, reminding herself not to show she was scared. Just like a grizzly bear, Sammi was more likely to attack if she smelled fear. It might be kind of hard to hide though, because with each step closer to the gym, she became even more terrified.

38

TRAINING

Rachael

MARCY STAR HAD to be at least a foot taller than Rachael. Okay, maybe not quite a foot. But the woman was a tower of muscle, and as Rachael stood staring up at her, she felt completely out of place and unworthy.

Of course, Belinda was the only other girl in her class. Rachael had tried speaking to her, complimenting her biker shorts. Belinda had corrected her. "They're called cycling shorts." She'd rolled her eyes and walked away. Rachael secretly wished she could go back to writing just so she could kill her off.

"Today, we're just going to get an idea of how fit each of you are," Marcy explained, smiling at the four students. Flint was standing behind her, his arms crossed, a cocky grin on his face. Across the gym, the other class was already hard at work doing calisthenics. Rachael desperately wished she had hit the gym a little more regularly. This just might kill her....

Marcy instructed them all to start jogging around the perimeter of the gym at a slow pace, and she'd let them know when they could stop and check their pulse. Each of them was wearing a high-tech monitoring device that made the Apple watch look like a wind-up number from a couple of hundred years ago. It would measure more than just their heartbeat. Rachael wondered if it would tell them how the sandwich she'd scarfed down right before class was digesting….

Her one goal as she started running was to do better than Belinda. The younger girl took off at a quick speed, her ponytail swishing back and forth as she went. Rachael assumed it had something to do with the guys in the other class. As they ran closer to where they were working out, she heard Sammi bark, "Eyes on me, losers!" Rachael turned her head to see that Sammi's eyes were on her, though. She swallowed hard and refocused her attention on Belinda's swishy ponytail.

Behind her, she heard wheezing and assumed that was Doug. The other guy in the class was one Rachael had met at graduation--Nick, the athlete—who was long gone having ignored Marcy's advice to take it slow.

Rachael seemed to remember that four laps around the gym was a quarter of a mile. She could run three miles on the treadmill at the gym before she felt like passing out, so she should be able to handle plenty of laps here, but there was something about the weight of Sammi's eyes on the back of her head, the fact that she was older than her classmates, and the indefinite nature of the run that had her lungs burning before she'd finished lap five. She couldn't remember how long she'd made newbies run, but she was beginning to think it was way too long.

By lap seven, Belinda was starting to fade a little. She'd clearly ran too fast to begin with. She was trying to make it look as if she was just fine, but Rachael could tell her side was hurting. Doug was sort-of walking with his knees bent. Nick had already lapped her twice and was working on doing so again. When he passed her, he always had something encouraging to say, so that was good at least.

"Keep it up, Rach. You've got this," Nick said as he flew around the outside of her, looking as if he'd already started his supplements. Rachael had one eye on Marcy, mentally begging her to please, for the love of God, say time. The other eye was on Belinda's ponytail. The swishing had slowed, but it was a nice distraction.

At lap twelve, her side had a hitch in it. How had she not even run a mile yet and was already feeling it? Luckily, she only made it halfway around before Flint shouted, "Okay--check your pulses, and head on over here."

Never in her life had Rachael been so happy to have a reprieve. Her heart felt like it was beating out of her chest, but when she checked it, the rate was only 97. So why did she feel like she was dying?

"Get a drink, and have a seat," Marcy instructed, gesturing at the water bottles they'd set on the perimeter earlier.

Rachael took a long drink of water, wiping sweat on the back of her hand. Doug looked like he was about to fall over. While Belinda dabbed at her forehead with her shirt tail, showing off her red sports bra, Nick was completely chill. He took a drink and headed back over to the trainers, and Flint asked him what he'd played in high school.

"Tight end," Nick said. "I could've gone to MU on a scholarship but decided to come here instead." He looked as if he wasn't sure that was the right decision.

"I'll say tight end," Belinda muttered, probably not realizing anyone could hear her. Rachael held back a giggle. She had a feeling Nick was too nice of a guy to want to spend much time with Belinda, despite her large rack.

Once they were all seated in front of the trainers, Marcy said, "Okay, what you all just experienced was an adrenaline rush and crash--well, maybe not Nick. It happens when you're anxious or nervous. Even if you're in good shape, it can happen. So our job as trainers is to get you in shape so that none of that matters. If you'll watch the other class for a second you'll see they're all wearing protective gear and getting ready to spar. We will be joining them for sessions later, once you guys are up to speed a little bit, so that we have more sparring partners. Look at their technique for a moment."

Rachael was awestruck, watching them combat one another, just as she had been the first time she saw it when Graham had shown her the gym. They moved so quickly, with such power and grace. It was difficult to believe she'd be able to do that someday. A look at Doug's face had her feeling sorry for him again. Defeat had settled around him. He'd probably quit soon enough if someone didn't step in.

"I know it seems impossible, but soon enough, you'll all be doing that," Marcy assured them. Then, staring into Doug's eyes, she reiterated, "All of you. Now, we are going to see how many sit ups each of you can do in five minutes. So, grab a partner, and decide who's going first."

Immediately, Rachael said, "Doug, will you be my partner?" The last thing she needed was to be paired with Belinda.

His eyes widened. Perhaps he was used to being picked last. "Sure."

She spun around so that he could put his weight on her shoes and waited for Marcy to tell them to start. At least there'd be a defined end to this, even if five minutes seemed like an awfully long time to do sit ups.

At Marcy's command, Rachael started her sit ups, ignoring Belinda the best she could, even though she secretly wanted to do more than the blonde. Doug counted in an encouraging voice, and even when her abs were burning, Rachael kept it up. She managed to do almost 300 sit ups in five minutes--five more than Belinda.

When it was the boys' turn, Nick blew Doug out of the water, but Rachael kept him moving, urging him on with encouragement while she counted. After five minutes, he looked like he might pass out, but he'd done nearly 200 sit ups, so that was something.

They moved through more calisthenics, including push-ups, jump rope, as well as kicking and punching so that, by the time the session was up, Rachael felt like her limbs were about to fall off.

Marcy and Flint kept them a few minutes longer than scheduled to be sure they knew how proud they were of their effort and then sent them to the showers. Rachael intended to grab her bag and head to her dorm to shower. The last thing she needed was for Belinda to flash her those perky teen breasts.

As she was headed into the girls' locker room, the office door next to it opened, and Sammi stepped out. Small, but mighty, she locked eyes with Rachael. "Barnes, can I talk to you for a minute?"

Regardless of the phrasing, it wasn't a question. With her heart in her throat, Rachael followed Sammi into the coaches' office, the door thumping closed decisively behind her.

3 9

NEVER GIVE UP

Rachael

SWEAT DRIPPED down Rachael's back, and she had a feeling it had
nothing to do with the fact that she'd just worked out for an hour and
a half. Sammi was standing in front of a cluttered desk Rachael could
only assume wasn't hers. There were six in the large office, but she
wasn't about to take her eyes off the trainer to glance around and try
to match her to a work space. She was glaring at Rachael, her arms
folded across her chest.

Rachael wanted to say something, to ask her what was wrong, or
what she wanted, or why she wanted her dead, but she had no idea
how she should address the trainer--miss, coach, something else--so
she just waited. The clock on the wall behind Sammi's head ticked so
loudly, Rachael could feel it reverberating in her fillings.

After what seemed like a week and a half, she finally said, "I don't
like you, Barnes."

Rachael raised an eyebrow. Commenting that she was stating the
obvious seemed unnecessary, so she held her gaze and waited for

191

Sammi to say more, trying not to show her emotions. Even though Rachael could already tell how the coach felt, it still stung to hear it.

Her face softened slightly after she made the declaration, and she moved her hands to her hips, which wasn't much better. "The problem is, I can't figure out why."

The sigh that came out of Rachael's lips probably confused her, if she even noticed it. Rachael was glad Sammi wasn't about to tell her that she knew Rachael was responsible for her sister's death. Since that's not what she'd said, Rachael was relieved, even though she still wished Sammi didn't hate her.

Rachael still didn't say anything, so Sammi continued. "You're a likable enough person. Everyone else thinks you're great. McCall won't shut up about you, and Graham's infatuated with you--"

"Infatuated?" Rachael said, taken aback. "I don't think I'd say infatuated…."

Sammi kept talking as if the other woman had never even opened her mouth. "It's clear to me you're not going anywhere, no matter what I think. I don't know if it's because my sister's fiancé can't stop drooling over you or something else. I mean, I didn't even realize that he had feelings for you the first time I saw you, but my immediate gut reaction to your presence was… pure loathing."

When she was done, Rachael waited a few seconds before she said, "Well, I'm sorry to hear that. I honestly have no idea why you would feel that way." Lies, lies, lies. "But… maybe once you get to know me, you'll see what a nice person I am, and we might even be friends."

To that, Sammi laughed. Loudly. "I don't have friends that are female, sweetie. I just tolerate other women because I'd get in trouble if I killed them."

Rachael knew that was true, too. "Well, maybe I can be the first." She laughed again. "You never know!"

"Yeah, no. I don't think so." Sammi's eyes penetrated Rachael for a few more moments before she rolled them and looked away. "But now that I've told you how I've been feeling, I'm starting to think maybe you're not so bad. I'm not gonna be losing any saliva over you like Graham…."

Now, Rachael's face was on fire. "Seriously, I don't think Graham has feelings for me. He hardly knows me."

Sammi leaned back so that she was sitting on the edge of a desk Rachael now realized had to be Ty's. There was a picture of him and what she could only assume was his mother on the corner. "All I know is, I've never seen Graham's eyes light up the way they do when he talks about you. Never. Not even when he was with Chell. And I hate that. Even though it's clearly not your fault. It's not like I don't want him to be happy. But, God, it's only been a few weeks. My sister hasn't even technically been dead a month, and he's already moving on."

"He's not moving on, though," Rachael reminded her. "Nothing is going on between Graham and me. If he's interested in me, and I'm not convinced he is, he's not acting on it. He talks about Chell all the time. I think I remind him of her, but he knows I'm not her."

"You remind him of her?" Sammi's nose wrinkled. "In what way?"

"I'm just telling you what he said." Rachael did her best not to scoff. Of course, Sammi wouldn't see it, but Rachael knew for a fact that she and Chell had a lot in common. She'd written her heroine that way on purpose.

"I don't see it. At all. You're nothing like Chell. My sister was an athlete. She was fast and strong. She was brave--not afraid of anything."

"I'm brave," Rachael assured her, getting a little feisty herself. "I may not be strong or fast yet, but I could be. Once I've had a chance to train."

Sammi was shaking her head. "I don't think you could ever be like Chell."

"Okay, but your sister was smart, right? And kind? She was funny and sarcastic. Witty? I've been described using those words."

She shrugged her shoulders. "Maybe."

"Listen, Sammi, I don't want to be your sister. And I'm not trying to replace her in Graham's life either. I'd be lying if I said I didn't like him or find him attractive, but I'm aware of his situation and would never press him to rush into anything so soon after such a tragic loss."

Sammi listened to what Rachael had to say, but she didn't seem convinced. "All I can say is, I won't be shocked if Graham ends up sleeping between your sheets sooner rather than later. And when that happens, you can guarantee, the last thing I'm gonna want to be is your friend."

"Fair enough," Rachael said. "But I don't see that happening." Of course, Rachael had seen exactly that happening in her head and in her dreams a thousand times, but she wasn't about to admit that to the assassin standing in front of her.

The trainer moved to the door and pulled it open. "Thanks for the talk."

Rachael gave her a small smile, thinking it wasn't as if she had a choice, and then stepped out into the hallway.

The conversation she had been terrified of for days was finally over, but she didn't feel nearly as bad as she thought she would now that it was finished. Instead, she actually felt like she might have a chance to win Sammi over after all. Unless the trainer happened to be right about Graham. Then, Sammi would want to murder her again. But if Sammi was right, and Graham really did have feelings for her, then at least she'd die happy.

40

SHE HATES ME

Rachael

THE FIRST WEEK of class went by quicker than Rachael would've thought possible. Whether the staff was busier because of the new students or Rachael just got lucky, neither Dr. McCall nor Sammi said anything else to her of concern. Anytime Rachael looked over to see Sammi glaring at her, she'd immediately stop, as if she wasn't doing it consciously. Dr. McCall didn't ask her to stay after again and complemented many of her answers in class.

Things were trucking along. Rachael started her supplements, and by the third day, she could feel changes happening in her body, mind, and even her spirit, which was odd since she'd never really been aware of that part of herself before. She was building muscle mass. Her reflexes were faster. And then, on Friday afternoon, while sitting cross-legged on her bed studying for a history quiz the next week, her pencil rolled onto the floor. Rather than getting up to retrieve it, Rachael closed her eyes, stuck out her hand, and willed it to come back to her.

Imagine her shock when it did!

"Get out of town!" Rachael screamed, popping up onto her mattress and doing a little dance. "Hot damn--telekinesis! The wonder of all super powers!" While she wouldn't have minded having the ability to read minds or fly, moving objects was a close third. The fact that she'd managed it so quickly was pretty damn amazing, too. It usually took students at least a month or two to have an inkling of a superpower.

She was just about to run next door and tell Jazz when her phone rang. Bouncing back down to sitting, she picked it up off the nightstand and immediately wished she'd used her new power. It was Ebony. They hadn't spoken for several days, so she answered it eagerly. Was it past 5:00 already? "Hey, Eb. How are you?"

"Not good." Ebony sounded more upset than Rachael had heard her in a long time--other than when she was mad at Rachael for not doing the job she'd already quit. "Something's really wrong with Frank."

Alarmed, Rachael pictured the middle-aged business man in her head and figured the only thing that could ever truly be wrong with Frank involved his tighty whities getting too tighty. "What do you mean?"

"I don't know, Rach. He's just been acting really weird the last few days. He's not been himself at all. His house was broken into a few nights ago. At first, I thought it was just because he was shaken up by that. But now... I think it's something else."

Rachael felt the hairs on the back of her neck stand up. "Broken into? By who?"

"They don't know yet. The cops are still looking. Rachael, there's been a lot of crime here recently, like more than usual. I've heard rumors that some gang has moved into town. Have you heard about the murders? Two houses full of people killed in less than two weeks. Lots more break ins."

"I've heard some of it." Rachael knew the two houses she spoke of where everyone was killed were linked to Sasha. Whenever Rex had finally gotten around to talking to Tripp about it earlier in the week, he'd said they'd look into it, that there was no reason to think it had to be Sasha. It could be a copycat. Rex hadn't been convinced, and neither was Rachael. Now, she wondered if Frank's break-in had also been vampire related.

"Frank said he was just glad the rest of his family wasn't home. They were out of town, or else they might've been killed. As it was, he said he was able to hide and call the police. They found him in the closet right before the police arrived and scared them off. If it was the same group that slaughtered those other people, Frank might be dead."

"Gosh, Ebony, that's terrible."

"I'm sorry to bother you right now. You don't have a class or anything do you?"

Rachael realized Ebony thought she was teaching, not studying. "No, no my classes are mostly in the morning."

"Good. Listen, he's in his office right now, and he's walking around, shouting to himself, picking up files off his desk and putting them back down. He keeps rubbing his neck and making a strange gurgle noise in the back of his throat. I'm glad it's almost 5:00 on a Friday, but I feel like I should go tell him to see a doctor."

"No, Ebony, don't do that. Listen, I know that Frank is more than just your boss; he's also your friend. But I wouldn't go in there." Rachael had to think of a reason to dissuade Ebony from entering the office of a potential vampire in an agitated state that would make sense to her. "I've heard that some of the other people whose homes have been invaded have been contaminated with some sort of... virus. You don't want to get sick."

Ebony was quiet for a second. "Don't you think I should go tell him that, then? Doesn't he need to go to the doctor?"

"Call him if you want to, but don't go in there. You've only got ten more minutes before you can leave. Go ahead and pack up your stuff, Eb, and get ready to go home for the weekend. I'd stay away from Frank until he's feeling better." She was definitely going to have to let Graham know about this. If Frank had been turned... there was a chance he could infect everyone at Merek and Merek and his family-- his wife and two teenaged kids. "I don't blame you for being worried, but really, Eb, you don't need to be sick right now. It's almost your birthday."

She sighed. "Aren't I just being selfish if I don't go take care of him?"

"Nope. He'll be... okay. Just head home, all right? Seriously, I've heard this virus isn't good at all. Tell you what, a friend of mine has a connection who can contact Frank and help him take care of it. He's a specialist in this field." She knew she was starting to stray away from believability again, but she needed Ebony to stay away from Frank.

"What field?"

"Viruses."

"So he's a doctor?"

"Yes... a communicable disease virus specialist." She wished she had come up with a better name than that. "I'll let the professor here know, and he'll give him a call. I'm certain he'll come see Frank. Probably tonight." The idea of Graham and his team busting down Frank's door and shoving a wooden stake through her ex-boss's heart seemed both ridiculous and heartbreaking at the same time.

"Well, if you're sure...."

"I'm positive, Eb. Go home, rest, and I'll call you tomorrow, okay?"

"Will you update me on the handsome man you mentioned before?"

Rachael felt herself blushing but was glad Ebony's tone had changed. "Yes, I will. So long as you promise to leave Frank alone. No matter what. Even if he comes looking for you, don't engage with him. Just... go home."

"Fine." Ebony was reluctant, but Rachael was fairly certain she wouldn't go back on her word. "I'm just worried. It must've been so terrifying to go through that."

"I can imagine it was." She could do more than imagine. She'd written plenty of similar scenes enough times, Rachael could envision them. "Go home, Eb."

"All right. Thanks, Rach. Talk to you soon."

"Bye." Rachael hung up, praying Ebony would be okay and she was wrong about Frank, but she had a horrible feeling she wasn't. This sounded like a vampire infection to her, which meant there was only one remedy, and it involved silver wood to the heart.

Without setting her phone down, Rachael dialed Graham's number. He answered on the second ring. "Hey. We have a problem. Can I talk to you in person?"

"Sure. I'm in the staff lounge right now, discussing a potential problem in Baltimore. Is this related?"

"Yes." She blew out a hot breath, glad he knew something but doubting he realized how close to home it was hitting for her.

"Come on down."

"To the… staff lounge?"

"Yep. I'm pretty sure you know where it is. You had an excellent tour guide."

"No, I do. It's just… it's the STAFF lounge."

"Come on down, Rach. It's fine."

"Ooookay. See you in a bit." She wasn't sure everyone would agree with that statement, but it would be easier to talk to as much of the team as possible all at once.

Rachael shoved her feet into her sandals and crossed to the mirror to fix her makeup and straighten her ponytail. She hadn't been expecting to go out again, but she tried to always keep up with her looks now, just in case Graham stopped by. Shoving her phone in her pocket, she headed out to go tell her new team that her old boss was probably a vampire.

A NOTE FROM THE AUTHOR

Thanks so much for reading Book 1 of Silverwood Academy. I hope you loved it and will be ready for Book 2, coming out soon.

Y'all know how I love writing about vampires and vampire hunters! I wanted to do something a little different with this one. Let me know your thoughts in a review on your favorite retailer.

Let's stay in touch! Sign up for my newsletter here:

https://books.bookfunnel.com/idjohnsonnewslettersignup

Please check out the rest of my books in the Also by ID Johnson page and check out my publisher's website where you can get several books for free at www.roguewolfpublishing.com

Thank you!

Immy

ALSO BY ID JOHNSON

Stand Alone Titles

<u>All I Want for Christmas is Pooch</u>

(<u>sweet contemporary romance</u>)

<u>Christmas Memory</u>

(<u>sweet contemporary romance</u>)

<u>Meet Cute Me Under the Mistletoe</u>

(<u>sweet contemporary romance</u>)

<u>The Doll Maker's Daughter at Christmas</u>

(clean romance/historical)

<u>Pretty Little Monster</u>

(young adult/suspense)

<u>The Journey to Normal: Our Family's Life with Autism</u> *(nonfiction)*

<u>Found by the Alpha (fantasy romance)</u>

Love Throughout Time

(time travel romance)

Back to Titanic

Back to Gettysburg

Back to Bunker Hill

Back to the Highlands

Back to Port Royal

Silverwood Academy

(paranormal romance)

Vampire Hunter

World Builder

Realm Jumper

Celestial Springs

(psychological thriller/literary fiction/women's fiction)

Beneath the Inconstant Moon

The First Mrs. Edwards

Leaving Ginny

The Motherhood

(dystopian romance)

Rain's Rebellion

Rain's Run

Rain's Return

Ashes and Rose Petals

(contemporary romance/retelling of Romeo and Juliet and Cinderella)

Girl in the Attic

Girl From the Tomb

Girl On the Beach

Nashville Country Dreams

(contemporary romance)

Meant to Marry Me

Lead Me Home

You Are the Reason

Forever Love series

(clean romance/historical)

Cordia's Will: A Civil War Story of Love and Loss

Cordia's Hope: A Story of Love on the Frontier

The Clandestine Saga series

(paranormal romance)

Transformation

Resurrection

Repercussion

Absolution

Illumination

Destruction

Annihilation

Obliteration

Termination

A Vampire Hunter's Tale (based on The Clandestine Saga)

(paranormal/alternate history)

Aaron

Jamie

Elliott

Christian

The Chronicles of Cassidy (based on The Clandestine Saga)

(young adult paranormal)

So You Think Your Sister's a Vampire Hunter?

Who Wants to Be a Vampire Hunter?

How Not to Be a Vampire Hunter

My Life As a Teenage Vampire Hunter

Vampire Hunting Isn't for Morons

Vampires Bite and Other Life Lessons

Gone Guardian

Death Does Not Become Her

Blood of the Vampire Hunter (based on The Clandestine Saga)

(paranormal romance)

<u>Night Slayer</u>

<u>Shadow Stalker</u>

<u>Queen Catcher</u>

<u>Mother Hunter</u>

<u>Father Finder</u>

Ghosts of Southampton series

(historical romance)

<u>Prelude</u>

<u>Titanic</u>

<u>Residuum</u>

<u>Lusitania</u>

Heartwarming Holidays Sweet Romance series

(Christian/clean romance)

<u>Melody's Christmas</u>

<u>Christmas Cocoa</u>

<u>Winter Woods</u>

<u>Waiting On Love</u>

<u>Shamrock Hearts</u>

<u>A Blossoming Spring Romance</u>

<u>Firecracker!</u>

<u>Falling in Love</u>

<u>Thankful for You</u>

<u>Melody's Christmas Wedding</u>

<u>The New Year's Date</u>

Charles Town Brides (based on Heartwarming Holidays Sweet Romance)

(Christian/clean romance)

<u>From This Moment</u>

Can't Help Falling in Love

It's Your Love

When You Say Nothing At All

My Girl

Unchained Melody

I Only Have Eyes For You

At Last

The Very Thought of You

Reaper's Hollow

(paranormal/urban fantasy)

Ruin's Lot

Ruin's Promise

Ruin's Legacy

When Kings Collide

(steamy historical romance)

Princess of Silence

Princess of Hearts

Collections

Ghosts of Southampton Books 0-2

Reaper's Hollow Books 1-3

The Clandestine Saga Books 1-3

The Chronicles of Cassidy Books 1-4

Celestial Springs Collection

Heartwarming Holidays Sweet Romance Books 1-3

Heartwarming Holidays Sweet Romance Books 4-7

Websites: https://books2read.com/ap/xX7ZD8/ID-Johnson

For updates, visit www.authoridjohnson.blogspot.com

Follow on Twitter @authoridjohnson

Find me on Facebook at www.facebook.com/IDJohnsonAuthor

Instagram: @authoridjohnson

Follow me on Bookbub: https://www.bookbub.com/authors/id-johnson